The
Rise & Fall
of a
Teen-Age
Wacko

The Rise & Fall of a Teen-Age Wacko

by Mary Anderson

Atheneum · 1980 · New York

"Laura" by Johnny Mercer and David Raksin
which appears on page 69, copyright © 1945,
renewed 1973 Twentieth Century Music Corporation.
Rights throughout the world controlled
by Robbins Music Corporation. All rights reserved.
Used by permission.

"You Can't Roller Skate in a Buffalo Herd"
by Roger Miller, which appears on pages 166 and 167,
copyright © 1964 by Tree Publishing Co., Inc.

LIBRARY OF CONGRESS CATALOGING IN PUBLICATION DATA

Anderson, Mary, date
The rise and fall of a teen-age wacko.

SUMMARY: Sixteen-year-old Laura who feels like the family misfit
returns early from the family vacation
in the Catskill Mountains and pursues her own adventures
in New York City.
[1. Vacations—Fiction. 2. New York (City)—
Fiction] I. Title.
PZ7.A5444Ri   [Fic]   80-12396
ISBN 0-689-30767-5

For Beano,
Mya-Pya
and r-r-r-r-Resa!

The
Rise & Fall
of a
Teen-Age
Wacko

Chapter 1

If a genie popped up to grant you three wishes, what would they be? To be rich, famous and fabulous-looking, right? Well, those would be my three.

And for a while this summer, I actually thought I was going to be granted one. The famous part. It was all sewed up. In the bag. Then, all of a sudden, the bottom fell out. And before I knew it, I'd made a fool of myself in front of half of New York City. It was even in the newspapers. Some of it, anyway.

I was, as they used to say in the movies, "a laughing stock!"

But I don't want to think about movies—not ever again—not after all the trouble they got me into.

I should've known it from the beginning. I should've *sensed* this summer was going to be a disaster. I wonder if the people who set sail on the *Titanic* sensed it

was going to sink. And do people who live near vol-
canoes get a twitchy feeling before they erupt?

Mom says I overreact in situations. But I didn't
overreact last summer when she first revealed our vacation plans. I under-reacted. The prospect of spending
an entire season in the Catskill Mountains didn't
thrill me.

When I was little, leaving the city for the summer
was terrific. But at sixteen, I no longer found it such a
big deal. Personally, I'd had visions of spending my
time roaming through Bloomingdales and exclusive
Madison Avenue shops. There's lots of other great things
to do in the city in summer—open air concerts in the
park, bike rides, sales at Bloomingdales.

Well okay, it's mainly Bloomingdales that inter-
ests me. Mom says I could live in that store and never
miss home. And it's true. I'm mad about shopping
and fashionable clothes. But to take full advantage of
all bargains, I have to do a lot of hunting around—
devote myself to shopping, you know. I've got to get
in the stores early, before things are picked over. And
summer's the best time to catch up on end-of-season
sales and plan a new fall wardrobe.

Since my birthday had just been the week before
the big announcement, I had lots of money—one hundred and sixteen dollars—burning a hole in my desk
drawer. I couldn't wait until school was finished, to
start spending it.

Everyone in my family knows it's "cash only" on

my birthdays. It's so much easier than returning everything to the stores later on. Mom and Dad hate the idea. "Money's so impersonal," they always argue. I don't agree. Cash is much better than three pairs of polyester slacks from Aunt Mona in Iowa, which sit in my closet until they're donated to the Salvation Army!

Of course, my little sister, Crissy, doesn't give cash. She's only seven, so she makes something. Usually a painted clay lump or a story about dancing mice. Mom and Dad always have a fit over whatever Crissy makes.

"Isn't she creative?" Mom will coo, admiring Crissy's latest sculpture lump. "She's taking after you, Kevin. (My dad's a free-lance artist.)

"Well, listen to this story," Dad will add proudly. "It's charming. I think she's taking after you, Margaret." ("Mom's a free-lance writer.)

I swear, neither of them carried on like that about the junky stuff I made when I was a kid!

But then, I've always been the misfit of the family. Not a creative bone in my body. Crissy writes her "brilliant" stories, illustrating them with tons of goofy little creatures. Mom rattles away at her typewriter all day, and Dad sits at his drawing board. Our apartment's crawling with homemade art and literature; but none of it ever smeared off on me. You see, I'm the superficial, materialistic one.

But I swear, with all the cash Crissy's got stashed away in her piggy banks, she could've broken her heart

and bought me a birthday tube of lipstick or something!
But, oh no, she won't even let me *borrow.* Once, I saw
this fantastic pair of designer jeans downtown. I was
only four dollars short. But that kid wouldn't lend me
one cent, even though I swore to repay her by the end
of the month.

"Mom says everyone should live within their
budget," she scolded, like some little old lady.

Did I mention that Crissy is precocious? Well, she
is. The brightest kid in her class. She started reading
when she was four. By six, she'd already decided on a
career—writing and illustrating children's books. My
parents were thrilled! Someday Crissy would combine
their two professions and follow in their footsteps. Crissy
already has a desk and filing cabinet like Dad and a
beat-up little typewriter Mom found in a local thrift
shop. She only pecks away at it now, but I'm sure it
won't take her long to learn to type.

Mom and Dad are too savvy about child psychol-
ogy to ever utter the unutterable phrase . . . "Why
can't you be more like your little sister?" But I bet they
think it.

While Crissy brings home report cards with notes
like "lovely child" and "brilliantly creative," I have to
settle for the same old line . . . "I hope Laura does
better next term."

It's awfully embarrassing, feeling inferior to a
seven-year-old!

And it's more than annoying having a sibling who

6

always agrees with all family decisions—no matter how *stupid!*

"Oh goody," Crissy squealed when she heard the news of our vacation. "The Catskill Mountains. That's where Rip Van Winkle lived. Maybe I'll see the little men bowling up in the sky."

"The rental agent said deer feed right outside the house," Mom added.

Crissy jumped for joy. "Will Bambi be there, too? I'll follow him into the woods and draw his picture."

Woods and mountains didn't sound at all appealing to me. I was more interested in clearances and thirty percent off!

"If we must leave the city, why can't we go to Long Island, the way we always do?"

Mom tossed me Section Eight of the *New York Times.* "Have you checked the papers lately? The shore's getting too expensive. We could buy a house for those rates. The entire summer in Windham will cost less than four weeks on Fire Island."

"Personally," I observed, "I'd prefer one glorious week by the ocean, no matter what the cost."

"'Well, your dad and I prefer an entire summer, thank you," she said, putting an end to the discussion. "And we're the ones who count the cost. Besides, it's settled. I mailed off the check this morning."

So much for living with democratic, liberal-minded parents!

Funny thing is, my folks are democratic about

most things. You can't survive on the Upper West Side if you're not.

You see, in New York, the East Side is known as ritzy, Greenwich Village is considered arty, and the South Bronx is just plain dangerous.

But the upper West Side is *everything*.

Artists, writers, businessmen, teachers and lawyers intermingle with winos, mental out-patients and various forms of addicts. Truly the melting pot. And most residents, like my parents, are proudly defensive of the neighborhood.

"I agree with Margaret Mead," Dad's fond of saying. "We must prepare our children for an unknown world. Growing up here, they're prepared for *anything*."

So you see, my folks are liberal-minded. They're active in both the Block and Parents Associations. Each spring, they help plant new trees in Riverside Park and are very proud of our ethnically balanced public schools. They go to all the museums, the theater when they can afford it, and are constantly extolling the virtues of living in the city.

That's why it's so ironic to watch Mom when summer hits. The moment schools have closed and the bongo drums begin pounding in Riverside Park, she's like a rat about to dive overboard!

And she's not alone. Anyone who can rub two pennies together begins making plans for the exodus. Many of my friends have summer homes, and the rest of the kids get packed off to camps. Even the boys disappear.

8

By the middle of August, our neighborhood looks like a ghost town. All you can see is an occasional husband or father whose nine-to-five job forced him to stay in the city. You can always spot him, looking like a zombie, forlornly dragging a shopping cart down Broadway, pinching plums in the local fruit store or fumbling through cans in the super market; never knowing whether to buy soup-for-one or the giant economy size. Pathetic!

So you see, the idea of actually staying in the city one summer would never cross anyone's mind. Anyone but me, that is.

I'd already started to fantasize about it. There'd be Bloomingdales, of course. But even I couldn't spend the whole summer shopping. I planned to catch some great old movies at the Museum of Modern Art. I'd even lined up a tentative job.

A neighbor, Mrs. Hallifax, who comes from England, has a neat little five-year-old named Sarah. Jessica Hallifax planned to take a refresher course at Columbia University, before going job-hunting in the fall. She wanted someone to sit with Sarah a few hours each day.

Now usually, I can't stand babysitting and only do it when my finances are dreadfully low. But Sarah's different. Very sweet, well-mannered and British, like the little girl Lewis Carroll modeled Alice in Wonderland after. I've seen photos of that girl and they even look alike. The best part is, Sarah thinks I'm terrific, too.

But that plan was nipped in the bud pretty fast. I didn't even bother to mention it to Mom; not after I learned she'd already sent off that check for the house in the Catskills.

We were going to Windham, New York, whether I liked it or not.

And I didn't like it.

Chapter 2

For the next few days, Mom went on her usual summer cleaning binge. She can't leave New York for a weekend, without things being in order.

The stove is taken apart and sprayed with poisonous fumes. The refrigerator is cleaned out, washed down and practically hermetically sealed. (There's always some hairy green thing, which was once edible, growing on the back shelf.) Cabinets are pulled apart. Flour, rice, crackers and everything else that might attract creepy-crawlies is packed in boxes, to be put in the car.

I swear, the woman gets crazed!

I never look forward to this scene, because I know it heralds bad news—the yearly clean-up of my room. The rest of the time, Mom doesn't care how messy it gets. I have the corner maid's room off the kitchen; so she just grits her teeth, closes the door and pretends it's not part of her apartment.

But come summer, the rules suddenly change. My door is flung open, and Mom presents me with a box of cleaning utensils—ammonia, Clorox, sprays, sponges. She dumps the box on the floor and leaves, but the message is clear—clean up, or else!

Okay, I'm a slob. But not totally. My clothing and cosmetics are neatly cataloged and organized. It's just the rest of my stuff that gets out of hand. Well, it's a little room and hard to keep in order. Besides, I like things all bunched up. It makes me feel cozy.

Once, I came home from school soaked with rain and opened my umbrella to dry it on my floor. As it happens, I forgot about and it stayed there awhile—quite awhile. I didn't mind. It was a little tough getting through the doorway, but who cared?

Mom did. She never said a word, but I knew it was driving her crazy. She'd pass by my room, stare down at that open umbrella still lying there, then raise her eyes heavenward and sigh. Lord, she must've told the entire neighborhood about it! I overheard a snatch from one of her phone conversations . . .

". . . No, Edith, she hasn't. Yes, it's still lying there . . ."

Of course, by that time, it'd become a matter of honor. I had to leave that darn umbrella out. Then one day, while carrying a pile of books, I tripped and fell over it and was forced to close it up. I never figured out who won that round.

That's the way it is with me and Mom sometimes— undeclared, unfulfilling combat. But when she hands me that box of clean-up tools, I know she means business. I guess I don't mind—as long as it's just once a year. It gives me a chance to weed out the clothes I never wear.

Actually, when it comes to clothing, the rest of my family are the slobs. All my clothes are neatly pressed and folded, while Mom spends most of her life in a pair of ripped-up jeans and an old shirt. So does Dad. Since they both work at home, it doesn't seem to matter. But I should think they're get sick of looking at each other, wandering around the house with India ink and typewriter smudges all over themselves.

Crissy's too young to be interested in fashion. So there's no one in our household to discuss the vital issues of the day: what colors are in and where my hemline should be. I could wear a burlap sack and no one'd notice. Or else they'd think it was the latest fashion and smile. "Very becoming, Laura."

They're in fashion's Dark Ages, both of them. I practically have to sneak my *Vogue, Seventeen* and *Glamour* magazines into the house under plain brown wrappers.

Do they want me to spend all my free time fumbling through libraries, the way Crissy does?

Is it a crime to want to look your best—to sample new lipsticks and lotions?

I know I'm nice looking, but it doesn't hurt to help things along, does it?

That's not how Dad thinks. "You're such a pretty girl," he insists. "You don't need all that phony stuff."

Phony! I'd hardly call four dollars per ounce phony.

See what I mean about being a misfit? I don't even look like the rest of my family. Mom is short and pretty, slightly plump, with a cute little-girl expression. Dad is short and dark. Crissy's inherited their dark hair, brown eyes and Mom's gremlin face. But I'm a throwback to another limb of the family tree entirely. I'm very tall, skinny (though I prefer to be called slender), with gray eyes and blond hair. I really look a lot older than sixteen.

Once, when Mom's friend Irene was visiting, she kept looking me up and down approvingly. "Really, Margaret, your Laura's turning into a beautiful young woman. Notice that aloof quality? Those high cheekbones? I wouldn't be surprised if she became a model someday."

I blushed with joy. My secret fantasy had been verbalized at last!

Mom blew some flour from her nose and dropped her mixing spoon in horror. You'd think someone had just suggested I become a fire-eater!

"I know Laura's pretty," she argued. "But I certainly hope she has something more substantial planned for herself."

You see how it is.

Chapter 3

By the time vacation day arrived, Mom had scrubbed everything in sight and packed enough boxes to get us through several winters in the wilderness. Of course, Crissy had to bring every fuzzy toy she owned, plus tons of diaries, notebooks, library books and her typewriter. That made two typewriters. Plus art supplies, pads and a foldable drawing board. Not to mention Dad's moped strapped to the top of the car. We looked like a bunch of Okies fleeing the Dust Bowl, and we hadn't even left the block yet!

"Really, Laura," Dad grunted, shoving my box of summer essentials into the back seat. "Must you bring all this gunk?"

"It's not gunk," I argued. "It's Jean Naté—moisturizer, after-bath splash and friction pour la bain. It costs a fortune."

And weighs a ton," he added, trying to find a free space beside Crissy's roller skates and molting animals. "We've got to jettison something. I can't see out the rearview mirror."

Mom tried to reorganize. "Crissy, perhaps you could leave some of your little-bitsies behind. Must you bring all forty-seven china mice?"

"I have to," she insisted. "I might write a book about them, called 'Country Mice.' But how could I write it if they weren't there?"

"Fake it," I said, grabbing her box of toys and placing it on the curb. This yielded enough room in the back seat for my hair dryer and makeup mirror.

"Oh no, you don't," she shouted, dumping them on the curb, staring at me defiantly, her hands crossed in front of her chest.

Crissy's short for her age and I'm awfully tall, so I tower over her. But she's a feisty little kid, who stands up for her rights. In fact, I'm always afraid she's going to bite me in the knees or something!

"I see the problem," said Mom, diplomatically. It's those inflatable rafts wedged by the window. Who packed those?"

"I did," I admitted. "We always bring them."

"To the beach, not the mountains, Laura," she said, dragging them across the back seat. "We've no use for them."

"You mean there's no water in Windham?" I gasped, feeling that someone had cut off my lifeline.

1 7

My parents know what a water freak I am. My entire summers are spent dipping and dunking. To confine me to a place that is waterless would be cruel and unnatural punishment.

"Relax," Dad reassured me. "The map shows lakes all over the place. But your mother's right. Some of this stuff's got to go, or we'll never make it onto the highway."

After several minutes of arguing, we compromised. Then Mom began packing a box of things to be taken back up to the apartment. Crissy's skateboard was the first to go. "I don't want to think of you careening down the mountainside," she stated. And my makeup mirror. "You'll have to survive without it, Laura." Being democratic, Mom forfeited her electric blender and Dad offered up his stash of art reference books.

While the repacking continued, Crissy desperately held onto Boris Baboon, determined he'd survive elimination. Boris is one of the first stuffed animals Crissy ever owned. It was given to her by some distant relative who must be demented. It's, without a doubt, the ugliest toy ever stuffed. Boris has a big plastic baboon face and a fuzzy body. At least, he used to be fuzzy. After years of being slept on, he's now matted down to mulch. But Crissy doesn't care. She still carries that thing around like an alter-ego. I think they're beginning to look alike.

After half an hour, one box of nonessentials had been removed from the car, along with one raft. The other was wedged under the moped for padding. Our folding bikes were jammed into the trunk. This left just enough room in the back seat for Crissy and me to sit uncomfortably. For three and a half hours!

After my stomach began rumbling audibly and my ears had popped several times, we finally arrived in Windham.

I must admit the view was beautiful. The house was literally on top of the mountain. And really deserted—off the main road, past a dirt road, up a private dead-end road, with no other houses around.

The hill sloped down for a clear view of the valley, including the whitewashed spire of a church steeple in the distance. It was surrounded by lush green mountains. Picture postcard stuff.

But the house itself must've been built by someone with a split personality. To best describe it, I'd call it a Spanish chalet. It started off stucco and Spanish at the bottom, but by the time it reached the top, it'd turned Swiss, with a balcony to catch the view of the mountains.

"What's that nice smell?" I asked, getting out of the car.

"Wild mountain thyme," said Mom, picking a handful of the little purple flowers. "Isn't it glorious?"

"Where are the deer?" asked Crissy, eager to begin spying on Bambi's cousins.

"Where are the keys?" asked Dad, eager to rest after the long ride.

Mom tore open the envelope the rental agent had

19

mailed her, unlocked the door, and we all took our first glimpse of the house we'd spend the next two months in.

Yes, it really was built by a split personality. The bedrooms were downstairs, and the kitchen, living and dining rooms were upstairs. I guess this was done to take advantage of the view from the upstairs terrace. It was great—an entire glass wall overlooking the mountains.

Otherwise, the house was typical of summer rentals. A scratched table here, sorry-looking sofa there, Aunt so-and-so's discarded drapes and gewgaw Christmas presents exiled to the "summer place."

While Mom examined the kitchen facilities and Dad wandered around looking for a suitable place to set up his drawing board, I checked the bedrooms. I wasn't thrilled to find there were only two. This meant sharing with Crissy, which I hated.

I could see it now . . . As I lay in bed at night, reading my fashion magazines, she'd be across the room, devouring Tolkien and C.S. Lewis. She'd have Boris propped up on the bed, his sappy simian face grinning at me accusingly. Well, maybe I could hang up a sheet or something.

But that wasn't the worst of it. There was only one dinky closet and one beat-up dresser. Quickly sizing up the situation, I ran to the car to get my things. I'd have to move into those drawers fast before Crissy claimed them.

But my kid sister's no slouch. When I reached the

hall, she was already in the doorway with her own boxes. She made a beeline to the bedroom and began un-packing her various toys, gangs of marbles and dozens of notebooks. By the time I returned, she'd already covered the dresser top with juvenile junk.

"And where, pray say, am I supposed to put my things?" I asked, glaring at her over my armload.

"I've left you a spot," she said self-righteously.

"Where?"

"That shelf down there."

Great! She'd left me the bottom rung of the night-stand. Just enough space for a pair of earrings!

"Very funny," I groaned, dumping my things on the bed. Clearly, I'd have to establish territorial rights immediately. "You take the bottom drawers. I'll take the top. You're the left-hand side of the closet. I'm the right."

"I've got no silly clothes to hang up. Just tee shirts and jeans."

"Then hang Boris in there. I don't want to look at his face, anyway."

For lack of a more brilliant gesture, Crissy stuck out her tongue and began moving things aside. "Being older doesn't give you extra rights."

"Maybe not. But being *bigger* does."

"Tell that to Goliath!" she said haughtily.

I swear, that little Munchkin always gets the last word!

But I decided to ignore her and finish arranging

my collection of *Glamour*, *Vogue* and *Seventeen*. Then I discovered what, for me, was the very neatest part of the house. The bathroom had a glass-enclosed shower stall and steam bath. At home, I have my own bathroom. But it's really tiny, with the sink in the bedroom. My tub's the old-fashioned footed kind, with plastic shower curtains that always whack me in the behind whenever I turn on the spray nozzle.

This was different. Tall glass doors sealed shut, and there was a cozy corner seat to relax on while the hot steam filled the air. I took a lovely, long, hot shower, then a glorious steam bath. Emerging forty minutes later, I covered myself with refreshing lemon lotion. Then I slipped into clean slacks and blouse and went to relax on the terrace.

A late afternoon mist was beginning to roll across the mountains. It looked strangely eerie, but was probably wonderful for the skin. Maybe the mountains wouldn't be such a bad place, after all!

While everyone else rode into town to find a supermarket, I continued relaxing on the terrace. There was a carpet of forget-me-nots growing across the lawn. And I knew enough about botany to spot the blueberry and raspberry bushes. There were also patches of camomile flowers growing around the bottom deck. Added to the scent of thyme, it made the air smell glorious. I was just recalling a terrific article in *Vogue* about homemade cosmetics, extracted from roots and berries, when the car pulled back into the driveway.

As I helped unload the tons of packages, I suddenly realized we hadn't eaten since breakfast. Dad had bought charcoal briquets for the barbecue pit out back, and we all began husking corn and making hamburger patties.

"I'm biking into town tomorrow," I said, feeling much better about Windham. "I want to check out the shops. These resort villages always have nice boutiques."

Crissy giggled, sticking her chubby fingers back into the bowl of hamburger meat.

"What's so funny?" I asked.

"Oh, nothing. You'll find out."

And I did!

The next day, after taking another super steam bath, I got on my bike and rode down the mountain into town.

I laughingly call it town, because it was, indeed, a joke.

Main Street consisted of a garage, drug store, small deli and a hardware store. Period. No nifty little shops or boutiques like in the Hamptons. Not even an antique store where I might find some old lace blouse or pretty linen hanky. The place was definitely dead or dying. In fact, I only saw three people strolling by, and not one of them was under eighty!

I continued biking, figuring Main Street had been

misnamed. Eventually, I'd have to hit a *real* Main Street. I had ten dollars of birthday money in a back pocket, and I was determined to spend *something*.

I passed a large golf course and several big Victorian hotels with luscious swimming pools. But all the people seated out front in wicker chairs were *ancient*. Seas of white hair or no hair at all. I mean it, I'd never seen so many old folks in one place before.

What could be going on? A Senior Citizens Convention? Well, they'd come to the right place. Windham was definitely not for swingers.

After I'd passed the fourth such hotel and seen my hundredth old person, I decided to give up and turn back. Of course, I'd forgotten I'd have to maneuver my bike back up the old dirt road, off the main road, toward the private dead-end road. It was uphill all the way. In the heat of the afternoon sun, I thought I'd pass out. By the time I returned home, I was ready for another hour-long shower.

"Mom, why didn't you tell me," I gasped, panting in the doorway.

"Tell you what?"

"This place is a refuge for the over-eighties!"

"I didn't know until yesterday. But isn't it sweet? I think it's wonderful old folks have a nice place to gather. Did you see all the old ladies wearing white gloves? And all the old men had ties and jackets."

"Yeah, very chic. I was hoping to find stores with

Sassoon jeans, but all they sell is denture cream and canes!"

"It's not that bad." She smiled. "Relax. Tomorrow, we'll all go swimming."

Chapter 4

I awoke next morning to an awesome sight!

Crissy was seated cross-legged on the floor beside my bed, her beady little eyes peering through me. A notebook in her lap, she was feverishly jotting things down. Then she'd stare at me again, mumble under her breath and write some more.

"Go away," I said sleepily, closing my eyes and rolling over.

"I can't. Did you know you slept with a sheet around your head?"

"The better not to see you with."

"And sometimes, you shove your head under the pillow."

"The better not to hear you with," I added, throwing it in her direction. "Quit spying on me."

"It's not spying; it's research. I've got to write a story about someone for the competition in school. And I might pick you."

"Don't do me any favors. Write about Mom and Dad instead."

"Maybe I will. Maybe I'll write about the whole family. Boris, too."

"I'm no relation to that baboon. Whose idea was this contest anyway?"

"Peter's. He says the best stories will be printed up, like real books. With jackets and everything."

I might've known! Peter came in to teach us when I was in elementary school, too. He was a really weird guy who just taught film making and creative writing. Once, he had our class drag video cameras up Broadway, to photograph the trash lying in the street. Then we had to write a composition about garbage and our souls or something. Really way-out stuff. But that's the kind of thing Peter thinks is *meaningful*.

"I hope you're not going to spend the summer taking notes on my sleeping habits," I said, stretching and sliding my feet into slippers.

"I might," said Crissy. "Sharing this room gives me the chance to observe things. Are you going to take another steam bath now?"

"I am," I said, grabbing my lemon cologne and shampoo. "And I don't want an audience."

"Peter says good writers have to observe *everything*. That's how they learn and grow."

"And die before their time," I added. "I'm sticking cotton in the keyhole."

My morning shower wasn't as refreshing as I'd hoped. There was a funny odor in the air, like rotten eggs. And when I got out, my body smelled of it, too. Even my hair seemed sticky and stinky.

"Mom," I shouted, running up the stairs. "Are you cooking eggs up here? An awful smell's coming through the bathroom vent."

"I smell it, too," she said, pouring some coffee. "I thought it was your father attempting to make breakfast." She sniffed her cup. "It seems to be everywhere."

"Don't blame me," said Dad, buttering a slice of toast, then rinsing his knife in the sink. "Margaret," he sniffed, "the water smells like . . ."

"Rotten eggs," I agreed. "My hair reeks of it. You mean it's in the water?"

"Well, this house hasn't been used in months. The pipes must be clogged with something."

"Should we let the water run?" asked Mom.

"Guess so. Keep the taps going today. That'll fix it."

Dad set his toast down and opened a large map onto the coffee table. "Join me in an expedition?" he asked eagerly. "There're lots of interesting spots around. Several lakes. First, we'll ride over to Jewett, then bike along . . ."

"Bike?" I said, dreading that trudge up the mountain again. "I want to go swimming."

"Then I'll go exploring alone. I'll bring the map and check out the surrounding lakes."

"Good," said Mom. "And I'll drive the girls to the waterfall. I noticed it on the way to the supermarket. It's only four miles from here."

By ten o'clock, Mom had parked the car on the side of the road, somewhere between Ashland and Prattsville, by a large sign reading Al's Motel.

"Is this it?" I asked skeptically. When she'd mentioned a waterfall, I'd envisioned some lush tropical rain forest, like El Yunque. This was just a rocky path off the highway. And we had to pass a burned-up tree stump with piles of garbage—rusty bicycle tires, beer cans, cardboard cartons and ripped-up clothing. "What a mess."

"It is awfully dirty," Mom agreed, holding Crissy's hand as we climbed over the debris. "But the falls are lovely."

Luckily, the place was deserted. Water flowed down the smooth slate rocks, ending in a stream, which poured into a small lake. We found a nice flat surface on the rocks and stretched out our towels. Crissy put down a face cloth for Boris to sit on, while I took shampoo from my beach bag. Then I plunged into the clean cold water and gave my hair another washing.

Crissy found a neat crevice in the rocks where

water cascaded down. Quickly discovering it was an echo chamber, she began singing "Teddy Bear's Picnic," while Mom laughed and wiggled her toes in the water.

I'd never swum by a waterfall before. It wasn't the ocean, but it was nice. After we'd taken our dips, we stretched out on the rocks for a lovely sunbath. I squeezed some lemon juice in my hair, hoping the sun would give it that naturally lightened look.

I was wearing my new copper-colored bikini, which I'd bought at Bloomies the month before. Though it looked good on me, I'd always dreamed of having a glorious tan from head to toe, without one strap mark intruding.

"I bet I could sunbathe in the nude here, it's so private." I sighed.

"You wouldn't really take all your clothes off, would you?" asked Crissy, about to grab that wretched notebook to jot down a juicy item.

"Not with Boris watching." Compromising, I lowered my shoulder straps.

"Next time, let's bring the raft," said Crissy.

"And the snorkels," Mom added. "This is so relaxing."

It really was. The sound of water gushing from the falls made us all feel drowsy. Soon, we were all stretched out on the rocks, almost asleep.

We must've lain there for about an hour before we heard it.

Transistor radios!

I looked up immediately. Scrambling down the rocks were about a dozen guys, loaded down with six-packs of beer. I could see their motorcycles parked above, beside the garbage-covered tree stump. (Now, I realized who'd created that garbage-covered tree stump.)

Living on the Upper West Side, I know creeps when I see them. And these guys were the genuine article! They were all wearing dirty jeans, cowboy hats and no shirts.

And their bodies were covered with tattoos—Satan heads, skulls, crossbones, snakes, daggers and wonderful little messages like HEART OF DARKNESS. A regular bunch of Hell's Angels!

They ran down the rocks, flipping open beer cans and throwing flip-tops in the water. Then they seated themselves in a row around us. The Invasion of the Body Snatchers!

I quickly sat up, pulled up my bikini straps and threw on my blouse. I poked Mom in the ribs, and I could see from her frozen expression she was as scared as I was.

Crissy grabbed Boris for protection, and all three of us sat there, waiting to be pounced on.

"Hey," said one guy, wiping beer foam from his moustache and staring through red eyes. "Ever been here before?"

Mom gave a nervous twitch. "Never."

"Swell place, huh?"

"Yes." She smiled weakly. "Lovely."

"Yeah," he added, turning up his radio. "Me and the guys think it's far out. That your family?"

Mom pulled us closer, the mother hen protecting her chicks. "My daughters," she explained.

"I dig it," another guy smiled, showing a gold front tooth. "Familysville. That's kinda nice."

"Mom," I mumbled, "let's get out of here."

Just then, a giant German shepherd came dashing down the rocks and began snarling at us. My heart pounded faster and I dropped my shampoo bottle in the water.

Another bare-chested creep, this one wearing large leather bracelets, grabbed the dog by its snout and pulled him away, just as its hot smelly breath reached my face.

"Don't worry," he said. "He won't hurt ya. Not unless I give the command. He's our mascot. Follows us everywhere."

"How nice," I whispered nervously.

"Go ahead," he insisted. "Pet 'em. He won't attack without my say so. But with the right command, he could rip your heart out."

A funny sound emerged from Mom—a squeaky gasp that stuck somewhere in her throat.

The Hound of Hell was once again approaching, his ugly teeth dripping saliva onto my knee. Somehow, I managed to get my hand thrust forward, dropping it on the dog's back, as he growled under his breath.

"You wanna pet 'em, too?" the man offered, pushing the beast closer to Mom.

Mom eyes glazed over, and she made the same robotlike gesture.

"How about the little girlie?" he continued. Dragging the dog by the neck, he presented him to Crissy. (Obviously, this guy wouldn't be satisfied until we were all equally contaminated!)

Crissy squashed Boris closer to her. "No!" she shouted, staring directly into the guy's naked chest. "Who painted all those pictures on you?"

"Like 'em, huh?" He laughed, glancing down at his arms proudly. "This one, she's a cobra. The other's a rattler. Cute, but deadly."

"I think they're ugly," said Crissy bluntly, foolishly unaware that these jokers held our lives in their hands.

"Hey, wait," another guy shouted, grabbing up my shampoo bottle, floating in front of him. "Been washin' up, huh?" he noted, throwing it into my lap. "Us guys do that, too. Every day, the gang rides over, has a few beers, then goes skinny-dipping."

"You mean you take all your clothes off?" asked Crissy with interest. (I'm sure she was wondering if those tattoos stopped at the waist or continued down their entire bodies.)

Mom and I signaled each other, afraid Crissy's remark might be considered an invitation. We gathered up our gear so fast we must've looked like figures in a speeded-up movie!

"Where are we going?" asked Crissy, about to open her notebook.

"Home!" I said, grabbing her arm.

"Now!" Mom added, grabbing the other.

As we climbed back up the rocks, a beer can came whizzing by above our heads, landing dead center in the pile of rubbish by the tree stump.

I didn't breathe a sigh of relief until we were all in the car, safely driving home.

"Let's not tell your father about this, okay?" said Mom, as we chugged up the bumpy dirt roadway.

"Why not?" asked Crissy. "Won't he be interested in our expedition?"

"Sure he will," I said. "That's why we should forget it."

Chapter 5

We arrived back at the house just minutes before Dad did.

"Remember what I said," Mom cautioned. "Not a word to your father. He's had a nice relaxing day exploring and I don't want it spoiled."

But as I watched Dad trudge up the mountain, pushing the moped in front of him, he didn't seem relaxed or tranquil. He looked hot, sweaty and grumpy as he maneuvered up the steep, rocky path.

"My legs are killing me," he puffed. "I got a flat a mile back. Had to turn around and push her home."

"Then you didn't go exploring?" Mom asked.

"Oh sure," he said, throwing himself into a lounge chair. "There's lots of lakes hidden around here. But you'd *have* to be an explorer to find them. Every one is *private*. Private roads. Private fences. Private driveways. I'm surprised they didn't have guard dogs to nip at my heels."

"We met a guard dog," said Crissy. "With big fangs."

"Never mind," said Mom. "You mean you couldn't go for a swim, Kevin?"

"A *swim*?" He laughed. "I could barely see the water. All this land around here's owned by camps, Margaret. But at least you guys went swimming. How was the falls?"

"Interesting," said Crissy. "But Mom wouldn't let us stay because of all the bums."

"They weren't bums, dear," said Mom, turning red. "They were . . ."

"Creeps!" I blurted out. (Well, as long as Crissy had spilled the beans, I felt Dad should know the sordid details.) "Just like Marlon Brando in *The Wild Ones*. Honest, Dad, it was right out of a movie. They were covered in tattoos and smelled of beer!"

"It wasn't *that* bad." Mom winced.

"Yes it was," I said, and digging further into my storehouse of movie knowledge, I added, "It reminded me of Tippi Hedren in *The Birds*. Remember that scene? She's seated on a bench with children singing in the background. Suddenly, hundreds of killer birds settle behind her, about to attack."

"Attack?" asked Dad. "Exactly what happened, Margaret?"

"They meant no harm. Laura's exaggerating. But when they spoke of taking their clothes off . . ."

"I thought *Laura* wanted to take her clothes off," said Crissy.

"No one took their clothes off, Kevin. They were merely tattooed skinny-dippers."

"That's right," Crissy added. "With a big dog to rip our hearts out!"

"Really gross, Dad. Not one of them looked like Peter Fonda."

"Sounds like a swell vacation spot." He sighed. "Guess you won't be going back there again."

I suddenly realized that that was true. Those creeps had robbed us of a perfectly wonderful swimming spot. And according to Dad, all the lakes were off-limits, too. That left us with nowhere to dip and dunk.

"It's not fair," I complained. "No stores. No beaches. Now we can't swim. What are we—prisoners on this mountain? It's like that awful movie with . . ."

Mom'd had enough! "Laura, get your father a glass of water. He looks parched."

Schlumping into the house, I stuck a glass under the kitchen faucet, which'd been left running. I don't know what came out of that tap, but it sure didn't look like water! It was rusty brown and smelled dreadful. I checked the bathroom tap, but the same brown gunk was pouring out. I filled a glass with it anyway, bringing it to the sundeck for closer examination.

"Sorry you didn't have a good ride, Kevin. No spots of interest?"

"Oh sure. But you can't get near them. Not even the shrine."

"What shrine?" I asked.

"Our Lady of Fatima. A lovely shrine, on top of a hill. But it had hundreds of steps. I couldn't drag the moped up, so I didn't go."

"Too bad." I sighed. "You could've prayed for water."

Dad frowned. "Laura, that's enough talk about swimming."

"I'm not referring to swimming in it," I explained, handing him the vile liquid. "I'm talking about *drinking* it."

"What's in it now?" sniffed Mom. "Rust?"

"God only knows," said Dad, "but we can't drink it. Keep the pipes running all night. If things haven't changed by morning, we'll call a plumber."

By morning, the water *had* changed. It wasn't rusty, brown or smelly any more. It was gone. We checked all the taps—no water in any of them.

Dad telephoned the local plumber, who promised to come as soon as possible. I had to forfeit my morning shower and my morning tea.

By noon, he still hadn't arrived.

Around three o'clock, Mr. Clampert pulled into our driveway. We all ran out to greet him like a long-lost relative.

"Hear you're having troubles," he said, dragging his tools from the car (and looking just like Percy Kilbride who played Pa Kettle in the old movie, *The Egg and I.*)

"We certainly are," sighed Mom, escorting him into the kitchen. "First, the water smelled of rotten eggs. Then it turned brown. Then it was gone."

Mr. Clampert nodded, checked all the sinks and plumbing, then went outside to examine the well pipe behind the house. He was still nodding when he returned a few minutes later.

"Seems your well's run dry. Folks up here on the mountain always have that problem." Taking a large bandana from his overalls, he wiped his forehead. "That's why there's not many folks up here on the mountain."

"Impossible," said Mom. "How can the town run out of water?"

"Town doesn't. You do. Can't pipe town water up here. Too high up. What you've got here is well water."

"But I heard it's always raining in the mountains," Dad argued. "How could we run out?"

"Sure it rains," agreed Mr. Clampert, chewing the last juices from a blade of grass. "Lots. And in six months, that runoff'll be in your well. Right now, you've got nothin'. Ya see, that well out there, she's three hundred feet down. When she runs out, you've gotta wait for her to restore herself."

"Six months," I groaned. "We won't even be here then."

"Won't take that long. Just a day or so. First, I've gotta replace your pipe. Burnt out. Shouldn't't've kept them taps running. That's what did it."

Mom and I gave Dad a dirty look, then she called the rental agent. He called the owner. The owner spoke to Mr. Clampert, authorizing him to make the necessary repairs.

By six o'clock, the work was done. But there was still no water.

"She'll come on slow at first," he explained. "Don't use her for a day or so, and she'll be good as new."

"I guess we can last without water for a couple of days," said Dad.

"We will if we have to," Mom agreed. "At least it won't be smelly and rusty any longer."

Mr. Clampert shrugged. "That smell, she stays. It's the sulfur in the water up here. Mighty good for you, they tell me. And that rust ain't rust. Red shale from the mountain. She stays, too. It don't look good, but it can't hurt you none."

"Oh no," I groaned. "You mean I have to shower every night in shale and sulfur!"

Mr. Clampert gave a folksy chuckle. "No, Missy. Don't mean that at all. Can't shower every night up here. No hosing, no watering the lawn; flush only when ya have to. And share baths, if ya can. See folks, this here is the lowest producing well in Windham. Be good to her, or she'll run dry again." Picking up his tools, he threw them into the truck. "Nice meeting you all. Have a real good summer." He smiled and drove off.

"Share baths!" I blinked. "That sounds disgusting."

"I won't mind," said Crissy. "I'll share with Boris."

Now it was my turn and Dad's to give Mom a dirty look.

"Didn't the rental agent mention this water problem, Margaret?"

"No." She sighed. "Only the deer and mist."

"Maybe Clampert's crazy," I offered. "He looked like Pa Kettle."

"I don't like being taken advantage of," Dad continued. "If there were problems, the rental agent should've mentioned them, Margaret."

"Yeah," Crissy agreed. "You got gypped!"

"You should've known better, Mom. Awful things always happen in the country. Cary Grant and Myrna Loy had a terrible time in *Mr. Blandings Builds His Dream House.*"

"Laura's right," Dad agreed. "So far, this summer's been a Brady Bunch rerun. And we've only been here two days."

Mom, sensing she was cornered, straightened herself to her full height, clamped her hands on her hips and turned crimson.

"Okay," she shouted. "Blame me for everything.

41

But if I ever do anything right, please let me know. Because it'll be the very first time!"

Then she turned on her heels, stormed into the bedroom and slammed the door behind her.

Mom didn't talk to anyone the rest of the day. We could hear her in the bedroom, pounding away at her typewriter, but she never came out.

Dad made some sandwiches and slipped them through the door. Crissy tied a note to Boris, which said, WE'RE SORRY, and left it in the doorway.

But I didn't do anything. I was still trying to recover from the shock of having to share sulfurized showers.

Anyway, Dad was right. So far, our summer *did* sound like a Brady Bunch rerun!

Two days of living on bottled drinks and going dirty passed painfully. When the water finally returned, it was, as predicted, both smelly and brown.

To avoid further arguments, Mom posted a schedule in the bathroom: one shower per person, once a week. Dishes were piled in the sink and washed only once a day, then rinsed sparingly.

I tried being philosophical. If I couldn't wash and couldn't swim, at least I could get tan. So, I invested the next week in lying on the sun deck. With my eyes closed, at least I could pretend I was at the beach.

But even that didn't work.

Crissy had discovered a giant clay pit down the road. Buried in the hard, caked ground, she'd unearthed all sorts of prints left behind by raccoons, rabbits, hedgehogs and deer. In only a week, she'd amassed a giant collection of them. And she kept them in foil plates scattered all over the sun deck. Every time I stretched out for a sunbath, I fell over some new crumbling fossil.

"Can't you move those mud clumps?" I complained, trying to find a resting spot for my brown lemonade. "I feel I'm in the middle of an excavation."

"No," she argued, "I'm doing research. Maybe I'll write a story called 'Mudballs of the Mountain.'"

"I've got a better idea, one that requires no research. Why not write one called 'The Day My Sister Slit My Throat.' I'll be happy to give you the details."

Dumping another armload of pie tins on the sun deck, Crissy rubbed her mud-covered hands across her legs. "You're bored. Only people with no brains get bored." With these words of wisdom, she skipped off down the lawn to pluck more strawberries with which to feed her face.

Well, she was right; I was bored. Yet, what was there to do? Mom and Dad were busy working. Crissy had her research, fossils and excavations. All I had was the sun deck. Getting a tan was fine, but turning into a prune wasn't.

I sighed, closed my eyes and tried to remove myself from the mundane world of Windham. I allowed my mind to wander to fashionable spas, expensive clubs and exotic places . . .

. . . Yes, an excavation, somewhere in the heart of the sunbaked Egyptian desert; where the treasures of Pharaohs were being unearthed. Not muddy pawprints, but rare samples of gold leaf, turquoise, alabaster and lapis lazuli; shaped into the most intricately beautiful jewelry, fit only for a queen. They'd lain in the silent stone beneath pyramids for centuries, their beauty known only to the earth. Goddesses guarded the doors of the tomb against intruders; ancient sentinels of the afterlife, protecting the exquisite treasures. But now, they were all lying scattered before my feet, placed by dutiful servants who bowed silently, exiting humbly back into their world of servitude. The gems were now gleaming in the sunlight. Their beauty was spectacular. The reds were like liquid fire, the blues as cool and deep as the ocean, the golds more brilliant than the sun itself . . .

"Lunchtime!" Mom shouted, interrupting my reverie. "Run down to the clay pit and get Crissy. And I hope she's not filthy. She's used up her water rations."

Throwing on my sandals, I fell over a clump of raccoon clay.

"Water rations," I grumbled. "This *is* like being in the desert!"

Depressed as I was, I realized I'd left one area unexplored—the woods. There were acres of them behind the house. Mom and Dad took long walks there each evening, but I'd never bothered. So one day, I packed myself lunch, slipped into some shorts and sandals, then took off: thinking it might be nice to run into a deer or two. I brought some fashion magazines, hoping to find a nice cool secluded spot where I could eat and read.

Following the long path behind the house, I entered the woods. It was still and silent, except for an occasional bird singing through the trees. Soft sunlight filtered across the ferns and everything smelled moist and new. Locust tree blossoms dripped with honey, and quaker ladies bent in the breeze. It was all so lovely. I was sorry I hadn't come before.

I guess I'd walked about a mile when a twig or something got caught between my toes. I leaned down to pull it out and suddenly screamed, throwing my picnic basket aside. It wasn't a twig at all, but a snake. A horrible brownish, greenish thing, crawling in and out between my toes.

Knowing nothing about snakes, I couldn't guess if it was poisonous or not. Would I have to cut open my foot and suck the blood out? The idea made me shiver.

Shaking my foot in the air frantically, I lost my sandal, which went flying into the bushes. Luckily, the snake hadn't bit me. It proceeded along its merry way, into the trees. But my lunch had been scattered all over. Already, a colony of ants was devouring my wedge of Edam cheese. And a bunch of flies had set up residence on my orange slices. My thermos was broken; my chocolate milk filled with ground glass.

And I couldn't find my sandal anywhere. I went burrowing through bushes to retrieve it, but it'd disappeared. The thought of walking home without it, with snakes crawling around, gave me the creeps, so I continued to look. My one bare foot kept squashing down on wet spongy stuff, which turned out to be mushrooms (which were probably poisonous, too).

But I had to find that shoe. I went fumbling through bushes and brambles, shaking loose grasshoppers, caterpillars, locusts—all manner of creeping, flying things. Of course, by now, my bare legs were scratched and bleeding.

But at least my Vogue magazine came in handy. I used it to swat away the bees swirling around my head.

I must've searched for that darn sandal for half an hour. I finally found it buried in the middle of a clump of ferns. But that wasn't all I found. It'd fallen on top of a large white mass. At first, I thought it was a giant fungus growth, but quickly realized it was a *skull*. (No doubt, the only remains of the last person stupid enough to wander through these woods!)

Actually, it was a deer's skull. There were several other bones scattered about—a leg, a hoof and various joints; all picked clean and dry. Except for a few red ants crawling through the eye sockets.

Some lovely nature walk, eh?

Then, of course, it took me ages to get back to the house, because I took the wrong path and lost my way.

I was fumbling around in that fungus-y jungle like a blindman for half the afternoon. By the time I returned home, I was filthy, scratched, sweaty, sore and starving.

But, at least I'd get some sympathy from my family when they heard about my horrendous experience.

Forget it!

After listening to the gory details, they were filled with comments.

"Laura," said Mom, "you should know better. Never go into the woods without slacks and sneakers."

"And always carry a backpack," Dad added.

"You found super bones and didn't bring them back?" gasped Crissy. "That's stupid!"

Insensitive. All of them!

Chapter 6

Well, it was back to being a prune!

I lay on the sun deck the next few days, soaking up rays and drying out several layers of skin.

Then the rains came.

And when rain comes to the mountains, it stays. Sometimes the mists were so thick I couldn't see the bushes in front of the house. At night, the fog rolled in like a giant cocoon, growing over everything. And it was hard to catch my breath. There was so much moisture in the air, I thought I'd grow fins.

Mom and Dad didn't notice it; they were so busy working. For them, the mountains had unleashed a spurt of creativity. One clattered away at the typewriter, while the other scratched at the drawing board.

Crissy didn't mind the rain, either. Or the fog. Or

the mist. It was wonderful background material for her stories. Presently, she was at work on an epic entitled "Van Winkle's Ghost."

As for me, I watched TV. One soap opera, followed by another. And another and another. Or maybe it was all one long soap marathon; I don't remember. Phoebe's drinking problem, Harriet's amnesia, Leonard's paranoia and Marsha's dual identity all got lumped together

I read my magazines from cover to cover, then over again. I polished my fingernails. And my toenails. Tweezed my eyebrows. Removed my cuticles. Pretty soon, there was nothing left of me to fix.

Whenever the rain let up, I'd wander into town and browse through the very limited selection of magazines in the drug store. I either had them, read them, or didn't want them.

Then I'd stop by the post office to pick up the mail from our rented box. There were usually checks and ads for Mom and Dad, and sometimes, a letter from Peter to Crissy. (I swear that kid'd written so much, I thought her fingers would wear down to nubs!) Once in a while, there'd be a letter to me from Gloria Goggins. Gloria and I are in the same class at school and live in the same building. I guess she's okay, if you ignore the fact she's a gossipy blabbermouth. Gossip is Gloria's reason for life. She's always on the phone, revealing someone's dark secrets. (The Goggins phone bill must rival the national debt!)

Anyway, the Goggins family has a house on Fire Island, and Gloria'd been sending me notes all summer. They were filled with disgusting details about every blond Adonis on the beach and every midnight swim party. They detailed each moment of sun-filled splendor.

One afternoon as I stuck her latest letter in my pocket, determined not to answer it, I strolled to the little library (actually, a one-room wooden house) where Crissy spent tons of time. But all the books seemed so old and picked-over, it was hard to find anything decent.

I managed to ferret out an Agatha Christie novel, buried behind some embroidery books. I was leafing through it, when I overheard the librarian (a wizened old lady, also over eighty) talking to someone. It was a young woman who'd come in with two small children.

"They say the rain's to stop tomorrow," said the librarian.

"Thank goodness," the woman sighed. "I'll take the kids to the lake. They haven't been all week."

"Lake?" I asked. "I thought all the water around here was private."

"Oh no," she smiled. "There's a lovely lake in Tannersville."

"Tannersville? Where's that?"

"Thirty minutes from here. You can get the bus on Main Street. It stops there twice a day."

"Thanks for telling me," I said, checking out my

book (hoping I now wouldn't need to read it). "I've been dying for a swim."

"It's called Rip Van Winkle," the librarian added. "It's man-made, you know."

I didn't care who made it. As long as I could swim in it!

The rain stopped the next day. When I awoke that morning and saw the sun, I began to feel much better. But my body longed to be submerged in water, and I couldn't wait any longer.

I called Trailways and asked for the time of the bus to Tannersville. Ten o'clock. Perfect. That left me enough time to dress and pack a lunch.

Feeling charitable, I invited Crissy to come along. The family was very impressed at my discovery of water, and Crissy couldn't wait to get her pudgy toes into the lake.

Carrying out food, towels and inflatable raft, we hurried down and caught the bus at Main Street. Half an hour later, we arrived in Tannersville. I asked directions to Rip Van Winkle Lake. It was only a short distance. We walked up a few hills, around a path, and there it was.

Water! There was even a little stretch of sandy beach.

Crissy and I ran toward it, threw off our clothes and jumped in. The bottom was muddy and slimy, but I didn't care. It wasn't the Atlantic Ocean, but I was content.

As Crissy dog-paddled around, I swam out a bit, to see the clusters of water lilies resting on the surface of the lake. Then Crissy went back to the beach to blow up the raft, and I lay on my back fantasizing about being in a tropical lagoon. I closed my eyes and let the world roll by. The water was soft and cool. Once again, the mountains didn't seem so bad. After all, the bus ride hadn't cost much. I could come every day to swim, if I liked.

And then it happened.

I suppose by then I should've been accustomed to having every brief idyllic moment of silence interrupted by some disaster. But I hadn't figured on this one.

Another *invasion*.

This time, it was little people. Dozens of them; hundreds, maybe. They came ballooning out of a wooden structure beyond the beach. Three- and four-year-olds mostly. They squealed and screamed then dived into the water with life jackets, rubber tires and tons of beach balls.

Before I knew it, the balls were flying over my head, little creatures were grabbing at my toes, swimming past my nose and screeching in my ears.

And two women were standing on the beach, blowing whistles, screaming out names:

"Claudia, don't push Denise!"

"Freddie, don't eat crackers in the water!"

"Patsy, stop throwing mud!"

I couldn't even see Crissy any more, there was such a mass of kids in front of me. Finally struggling loose from the hands that clutched my foot, I caught a glimpse of her floating along on the raft. There were nine other little kids hanging off the side, with another six dangling from the ropes.

"Gosh, this is fun," she squealed, floating past me. "You didn't tell me there'd be other kids. Meet my new friends. They all belong to Camp Wachanawa."

So that was it. I was swimming right in the center of a kiddie camp. Wachanawa! (Some long-dead Indian's revenge on the White Man, no doubt!)

Struggling from the water, I dislodged several little hands still clinging to the back of my bikini. Drying myself off, I approached the camp counselor, just in time to have her blow the whistle in my ear.

"How long is camp in session?" I asked, hoping she'd say they were all grabbing a boat for Russia any minute.

"Everyday," she smiled. "Ten to five. All summer long."

"Terrific," I groaned.

"Have a little brother or sister who'd like to join?"

I didn't answer. I returned to my beach towel, hoping to drown my disappointment by eating lunch on the sand.

But by now, our lunch was sand. Those creepy little kids had trampled all over it. The sandwiches were squashed and gritty, the peaches turned to mush. And yes, another thermos had been knocked over. This one wasn't broken, but the juice had spilled all over the place.

Crissy was having a great time. She splashed around in the water with her newfound friends, happy as a clam. At last she'd found an entire race of people shorter than she was! I couldn't even drag her out long enough to check on the bus schedule back to Windham. So I asked the counselor to keep an eye on her while I walked back to town.

The man in the candy store gave me the next bit of bad news. The next bus returning to Windham was at four thirty. This meant we were stuck in Tannersville for several more hours. I'd only brought bus fare, so I couldn't buy us food.

Crissy didn't care about that, either. Her new friends had shared their snacks with her. When I returned to the beach, a gang of them had just polished off several bags of chips, Doodles and peanuts. And she'd never thought to save me one.

For the rest of the afternoon, I was treated to the glorious strains of a zillion kids singing the Camp Wachanawa song. When one batch of little folk had finished swimming, they charged back into the wooden building, to be replaced in the water by yet another batch.

54

Those inside had hobby hour. They pounded and banged away with hammers and wood, singing at the top of their little lungs.

By this time, Crissy was in seventh heaven. "See what I built?" she said, shoving a hunk of wood with nails hanging off it into my face. "It's a bed for Boris."

"Wonderful," I said, checking my watch. It was only three o'clock.

Then came another snack period. This time, I managed to steal a few crackers from a kid who left them on the picnic table. (He looked overweight, anyway.)

When four fifteen arrived, I couldn't wait to catch the bus. Dragging Crissy away, she bid a fond farewell to her friends, promising to see them all again.

"Can I come again?" she asked the counselor, pleadingly.

"Anytime. This camp's free to all summer residents."

"Aren't I lucky?" Crissy beamed. "Will you bring me back tomorrow, Laura. Please."

"Don't hold your breath."

Riding back home, Crissy was so exhausted, she fell asleep. I woke her when we got to Main, and the first words from her mouth were, "Can I go back with you again tomorrow, Laura? Please, can I?"

I'd never seen her plead like that before. She looked almost—well, *vulnerable*.

"I don't think I could take it, Cris. But listen,

talk to Mom and Dad. Maybe you're big enough to take the bus by yourself."

Her eyes turned to saucers. "By myself? Wow, that's even better!"

Chapter 7

Crissy didn't waste a minute. That evening, she begged Mom and Dad to let her go to Camp Wachanawa. Alone. At first they refused, insisting she was too young to travel by herself. Mom offered to chauffeur her back and forth. But Crissy was insistent. (Since I'd put the germ of independence in her head, she was hanging onto it.)

"I'm too big for that," she argued. "The camp's real easy to get to. I can go by myself."

The next morning, Mom decided to check it out. She and Crissy waited on Main Street for the Trailways bus. Mom spoke to the driver, Jerry Lowell, and discovered he worked the route back and forth every day. Jerry promised to keep an eye on Crissy, swearing not to leave Tannersville without her. Reluctantly, Mom decided to give it a try.

At five o'clock, we were all waiting on Main Street for the bus to return. Crissy climbed off, sunburned and smiling.

"I had a great time," she yelled. "There were lots of old ladies on the bus, both ways. They said I'm cute. Jerry thinks I'm cute, too, don't you?"

Jerry tipped his hat. "See you tomorrow, Cris." He smiled, then drove away.

"Well, I guess that's settled," said Mom. (I think she felt a little uneasy, having nothing to worry about.) "I guess my little girl is growing up."

From then on, even on rainy days, Crissy went to Camp Wachanawa. She made lots more furniture for Boris, a woven placemat for Mom, and a penholder for Dad.

At first, I was thrilled to have her out from underfoot. But I still had nothing to do. Now, I didn't even have someone to shout at.

Mom and Dad continued working like beavers, and I read every Agatha Christie novel the library had to offer. My one hundred and twelve dollars was about to burn a hole in my dresser drawer. There was still more than a month of summer left, and I knew I couldn't last.

That's when I got my brilliant idea!

If Crissy could travel on Trailways alone, I certainly could, too. Not to Tannersville, of course; I never wanted to see that place again.

That evening, I got out my phone book and called New York City.

"Mrs. Hallifax? This is Laura Andrews. How are you?"

"Fine, Laura. I thought you were on vacation."

"I am. How's your class at Columbia?"

"Most interesting. But I can't complete the last two weeks. Sarah's aunt's been looking after her, but she's going to Florida tomorrow."

"Then you still need a babysitter?"

"I surely do. But everyone seems to be out of town. You don't happen to know anyone, do you, Laura?"

"I might, Mrs. Hallifax. I'll call you back tomorrow and let you know."

That evening, I set the wheels of my plan in motion.

First, I cleaned my half of the room. Then I washed all the dishes. I even made dessert for everyone. I brought Mom and Dad their coffee, and as they were sitting, relaxed and receptive, I made my move.

"Crissy, you're sure having a great time at camp,"

I said casually. "I bet you love being on your own and independent."

"Yeah. Riding the bus alone is easy. I've made lots of new friends, too."

"Yes," said Dad, "it's been great for you."

I made my second move. "All children should have an opportunity for independence, don't you agree, Dad?"

"Certainly," he said, browsing through the newspaper.

"Especially *teenagers*, don't you agree, Mom?"

"Certainly," she echoed, leafing through a magazine.

"I'm glad you both feel that way. Because I'd like to return to New York. *Alone*."

They dropped their newspaper and magazine in unison.

"*What are you talking about?*"

"I've checked the bus fare," I continued. "It's only fifteen dollars. I'll take it from my birthday money; I don't mind. And I'll only need a few dollars for food and carfare in the city. You'll give me that, won't you? I won't eat very much, I promise."

"Don't be silly," said Mom, assuming that ended the conversation.

"It's lovely here." Dad sighed. "The mountains, the woods . . ."

"It's boring!" I shouted. "I hate the fog, the

60

snakes, everything. In fact, I think I may be going crazy!" (I hadn't meant to lose my cool like that. I'd planned a reasonable, intelligent discussion.)

Mom stared at Dad, then at me.

"I didn't know you were unhappy here. I guess we've been so busy, we didn't notice. But going to the city all alone; that's no solution."

"I'll come with you," Dad offered. "I can finish up my work there, as well. I won't mind."

"You don't understand," I continued. "I want some time by myself. After all, I'm sixteen."

"But it doesn't make sense, honey," Mom argued. "You'd be all alone with nothing to do."

"I've a job," I announced. "Mrs. Hallifax wants me to sit for Sarah. She'll pay two dollars an hour. That's thirty dollars a week! And I want to do it, Mom, please!" (I realized I now sounded exactly like Crissy. I only hoped I looked as vulnerable!)

They shrugged their shoulders, still not taking to the idea. That's when I made my third move and changed my approach. I'd appeal to their liberal minds.

"Oh, I see," I said coolly. "You don't trust me, is that it? You don't think you've raised a daughter who knows how to take care of herself."

Bingo! I could see Dad was weakening.

"Nonsense. Of course you can. As Margaret Mead said, we must raise our chil—"

"That's not the point, Kevin. You watch the Late

Night News. Horrible things happen to young girls alone in the city. They wind up lying on their living room floor in a pool of blood!"

"I'll lock and double latch the door each night, I swear."

"Well," said Dad, clearly disturbed by Mom's graphic example, "we'll have to think about it."

"What's to think about? Can I go or can't I? What's the verdict?"

"Oh goody," Crissy suddenly piped up. "We all get to vote. Let's write them on little papers and put them in a bowl."

"Mom and Dad'll decide this," I snapped. "I promise not to go out at night. And I won't cook, so don't worry about me burning the place down."

Crissy giggled. "You *can't* cook."

"That's right," Mom agreed. "And you have to eat."

I smiled, pleased I'd thought of everything. "Fresh fruits, raw vegetables, cereals, milk and juices. A perfectly balanced diet."

Dad looked pensive. "How long would you want to stay?"

So, far, so good.

"Mrs. Hallifax needs me for two weeks."

"Two weeks!" Mom gasped, making it sound like two years. "That long?"

"It's not long at all. I'll be back before you know it."

"You'd have to find a place to put your money," Mom warned. "I don't want to worry about your being mugged."

"You can have my secret place," Crissy offered. "I stick my coins in my mouth, so I never lose them."

Mom frowned. "Crissy, you put money in your mouth? That's disgusting."

"No it's not. I wipe them off before I pay."

I could see the discussion was getting off the track. "I won't put money in my mouth, I promise. So what do you say?"

"Well, I guess so," said Mom uneasily.

"Yes," Dad agreed. "I guess so."

I could hardly wait for morning to arrive. I was up at the crack of dawn, packing. It seemed an eternity before ten o'clock came. I must've checked my money purse a dozen times. Hard to believe I was only hours from Manhattan and all its delights.

Mom gave me food money, two sets of keys (in case I lost one), sandwiches to eat on the bus and enough advice to last a lifetime. I listened to it all, nodding politely. Dad kept talking about Margaret Mead and how confident he was I was facing new challenges. They really must've thought I was going to Siberia!

But I didn't mind. I didn't even care that I had

to share the bus ride with Crissy as far as Tannersville.

That part was almost too much for Mom. When she saw *both* her little girls getting on the bus for "the unknown," I thought she was going to cry.

"Don't worry, Mom, I'll be fine."

"Of course you'll be fine." She smiled, stifling a whimper. "We know that. You know she'll be fine, don't you, Kevin?"

"Yes, Margaret. She'll be fine."

"See that. Nobody thinks you won't be fine."

"Call us when you get into town," Dad added. "And don't forget to double latch."

I nodded, smiled and waved one last goodbye. As the bus pulled out, Mom stretched out her arms. For one horrible moment, I thought she might attach herself to the rear, dragging herself along to New York City.

But in a moment, they were both pinpoints in the distance.

Crissy settled down next to me, munching a candy bar. "It's nice traveling alone. Wait and see. You'll like it."

"I know I will." I sighed.

I stared down the tree-lined road, taking me closer and closer to Manhattan.

Chapter 8

The ride was wonderful, and time passed quickly.

Why hadn't I thought of this sooner? Suddenly, I realized what little independence I'd had; never traveling anywhere alone. At my age, that was inexcusable.

Oh well, today Manhattan; tomorrow, who knew.

It was two o'clock when the bus pulled into the Port Authority Terminal. Within minutes, I was caught in the crunch of hundreds of people and realized something else. I hadn't seen so many humans in a month. Being deserted on a mountain so long, they took getting used to again.

Stepping onto Eighth Avenue, I sniffed the air. It smelled like burned rubber. Something else to get used to. For a moment, I considered splurging on a taxi, then realized I'd have to stop on Broadway for groceries, anyway. I reentered the terminal, dragged my suitcase down the ramp to the IRT subway and took the train to Ninety-sixth Street. There, I went in the corner supermarket to pick up some food. I bought milk, strawberries, cereal, raisin bread and ginger ale. Then I stopped at the newsstand to pick up the latest fashion magazines and a *TV Guide*. (I hoped there'd be some wonderful vintage movie on later that night.)

Reaching my building on Riverside Drive, I noticed that Larry, our doorman, wasn't in the lobby—probably taking a coffee break. I fumbled through my bag for the key, making sure to lock the entrance door behind me. The empty lobby seemed a little creepy. I took the elevator upstairs and unlocked the door to my apartment.

We live in an old building, broken up into two separate sides, with two apartments per section. Our next door neighbors are opera singers who spend most of their time traveling in Europe, so we have the entire floor to ourselves. Normally, it's ideal privacy, but just then it seemed awfully deserted.

I pushed open the apartment door. It was darkly silent inside. And empty. I'd never seen it so empty. Whenever I'd come home from school, either Mom or Dad were there. Mom had an early schedule—up at six and into bed by eleven. Dad liked sleeping till noon and working late at night, So, night or day, someone was always cooking, cleaning, writing or painting somewhere.

Except now, of course. Now it was all mine. And it seemed strangely unfamiliar. There was a musty odor in the air, too.

I walked down the long, dark hall toward the pantry. Even the monotonous buzz from the freezer was absent. After plugging it in, I put away my groceries.

Yes, the apartment definitely seemed strange. Ghosts of Mom, Dad and Crissy clung to everything. A jacket thrown over an easy chair gave me a fright. I thought the arm hanging over the side had someone in it!

Before doing anything else, I called my parents. Hearing their voices reassured me. After all, they were only a phone call away.

I took off my sticky clothes and prepared to get into an hour-long shower in unsmelly water. Unfortunately, images of Janet Leigh in *Psycho* drove me from the bathroom much sooner than I'd planned!

I wandered around, opening windows in some rooms, turning on air conditioners in others; trying to rid the place of its stale, closeted odor. There wasn't a sound in the building. Could I be the only one there? Maybe I was, except for the zombie nine-to-five husbands who hadn't returned from offices yet. This idea didn't thrill me. The building was crying out to be burglarized!

Then I remembered Mrs. Hallifax. I called to

give her my news. She was thrilled to learn I'd be baby-sitting and asked me to come at nine o'clock the next morning.

Still, I felt uneasy. So I got dressed again, went up to Broadway and bought some garlic and onions. To wear around my neck and scare off intruders? No, I had a better idea. Once Mom'd told me about a friend of hers who hated cooking. Each night, she'd fry up some onions, then pop a TV dinner in the oven. When her husband came home, the oniony smell filled the kitchen and he always thought he'd be eating something grand. All she did was dump the onions on the TV dinner, but he didn't care. The smell was what got him.

So that's what I did, too. I fried up a mess of garlic and onions, then shoved them in the frig. The smell made the apartment feel homey and lived in. (And it'd ward off any burglar who came sniffing at my door!)

It worked. I felt much better.

I opened the *TV Guide* to check the film listings. I was thrilled. The movie, *Laura*, was scheduled for six o'clock. Though I'd seen *Laura* five times, I never missed a chance to see it again. It'd been Mom's favorite movie when she was younger, too. In fact, that's where I got my name.

Mom'd been wild about Gene Tierney who played the title role. And the character, Laura Hunt, had been Mom's inspiration: a young, beautiful, talented, successful career woman, adored by everyone; able to make men fall in love with her, even from the grave. Just one look at Laura's beautiful portrait and men's hearts were lost.

Mom even knew the movie's theme song by heart. And so did I.

Laura is the face in the misty light
Footsteps that you hear down the hall
A laugh, that floats on a summer's night
That you can never quite recall

And you see Laura
On the train that is passing through
Those eyes, how familiar they seem
She gave her very first kiss to you
That was Laura
But she's only a dream

Gosh, they don't write romantic songs like that anymore!

Going into the kitchen, I hummed the tune to myself; anxious to see the film again. I took my delicious basket of strawberries from the frig, rinsed them off and put them in Mom's best cut crystal bowl. I poured some ginger ale into Mom's finest long-stemmed champagne glass and put them both on our fanciest silver tray. Taking a lace-edged hanky from the sideboard, I slipped it onto a corner of the tray. Then I carried it all into my parent's bedroom and placed it beside the TV. (No sense sleeping in my dinky bed when I could have a queen-sized one.)

By now, I was really in the mood to watch the movie. As I stretched out waiting for it to begin, I began to fantasize about Laura Hunt.

. . . Laura, impeccably dressed, beautifully made up, traveling through the posh offices of Madison Avenue, carrying a portfolio. Of course, mine wouldn't have art sketches in it, like hers. Mine'd be filled with tons of modeling shots.

. . . Laura Andrews—New York City's highest paid, most in-demand model. Laura Andrews, who traveled across the globe, wearing designer clothes and meeting fascinating people. I'd be admired, fawned over, fallen madly in love with. I'd be draped in the sheerest silks, the softest leathers, the subtlest scents, the finest jewels. I'd stand barefoot and laughing in Grecian fountains. I'd stroll down cobblestoned London streets in perfectly tailored tweeds. I'd ride horseback through the salty surf of the Bahamas. *And I'd get paid a hundred bucks an hour!*

Was it such a fantasy? I didn't think so. I was tall, slender and (according to everyone) very pretty. I'd spent hours at my mirror, analyzing all my features: long eyelashes, good cheekbones, well-shaped lips and an upturned nose. What more was needed?

After all, being a model was probably a fantasy to Cybil Shepherd and Cheryl Tiegs once!

Suddenly, I felt stupid having such "superficial" thoughts, stretched out there in my parent's bedroom. Mom's photo stared at me from the dresser. What would she say if she could read my mind? . . . "Laura dear, get your head out of the clouds. Plan something solid for your life."

I couldn't help it. A hundred bucks an hour sounded awfully solid to me!

I popped a strawberry in my mouth, switched on the TV, and cuddled under the covers. Soon, the strains of *Laura's* theme song filled the room.

Maybe it was fantasyland; but I loved it.

Chapter 9

I slept like a baby, visions of fashion models dancing in my head. I had such wonderful dreams, I almost didn't hear the alarm go off. I got up, made myself raisin toast and tea, then took a lovely long shower.

Refreshed and confident, I arrived at Mrs. Hallifax's apartment at nine on the dot. I'd barely gotten in the door when Sarah popped from her room and waved me inside·

"Laura," she said, "come see what I've done."

"She's having a tea party for her dollies," Mrs. Hallifax explained, grabbing her books. "See you at noon."

"Hurry, Laura," said Sarah excitedly.

Sarah has a nifty little girl's room, complete with canopied bed, dripping organdy ruffles all over the place. Disgustingly feminine, but it suits her. And she has a terrific doll collection.

I guess all kids with divorced parents wind up with lots of loot, but Sarah's toys are really spectacular. Her father sends them from England, and I think they're all antiques. She has lots of old-fashioned bisque dolls with yards of lacy dresses. Several were seated on tiny wooden chairs around a small oak table set with a miniature china tea service. There was real tea in the pot and a plateful of tiny toast sections and little jars of raspberry jam and marmalade.

"I told them you were coming," she said. "They've been very polite and haven't started eating yet."

I curtsied, pulled up a chair and began pouring the tea. "What are your guests' names?"

Sarah giggled. "That's Prudence in the straw hat. Penelope's wearing the fur cape. Eliza's in the middle. Mary's on the end. And that's Lavinia. She's been naughty today, but I let her come anyway."

"Shall we spread some sick-mary on her toast?" I asked.

"That's marmalade," Sarah corrected.

"I know it, but that's what marmalade means. I read it in a book. When Mary Queen of Scots was exiled to Scotland, she got very sick and asked for oranges to be shipped from France. To preserve them, they made them into a jam called marmalade—sick-mary, you see?"

Sarah was thrilled at my fountain of knowledge. "Then Mary shall have some sick-mary, too. Even though she gets it on her face."

We had a lovely tea party, then Sarah helped me

rinse the things and put them in her dollie cabinet. I read her the last two chapters of A *Little Princess* (where Mrs. Hallifax had left the bookmark), then we started *Bambi*. After some chapters of that, I told her stories about all the deer we'd seen in Windham, its beautiful woods and lovely mountain mist. (I lied a lot, but the kid enjoyed it!)

The time went so quickly, Mrs. Hallifax was back before I knew it. I'd made six dollars. Painlessly.

I said goodbye to Sarah, looking forward to seeing her the next day. Then I was off to Bloomingdales, where I immediately hit pay dirt! All the lovely silk skirts and blouses I could only swoon over in June were now on sale. And the beach hats, camisoles, zippy tee shirts—everything was marked down. I'd brought fifty dollars, and it'd go further than I'd thought.

I could hardly wait to try things on. As usual, I took some fancy gowns into the dressing room, just for fun. I love trying on elegant clothes, even if I can't buy them. But when the serious job of selection arrives, I'm more practical. I choose neutral colors that match each other, stretching a few things into several different outfits.

Trying on is half the fun. Just the smell of new clothes and the crisp touch of them makes me feel good. And I love reading the tags—dry clean only, wash in warm water, tumble dry—friendly little messages about the care and feeding of fine clothing. And I always obey.

74

For a moment, I was tempted by a lacy purple gauze swirl skirt, then rejected it. It wouldn't match anything. But the beige silk wraparound would, and the price'd been slashed. I reread the tag three times, hardly believing it. With the money I'd saved, I could afford an extra top; maybe two. Finally, I decided on the cocoa silk blouse and the chocolate cotton shirt.

I paid the cashier. For the first time in my life, I was leaving Bloomies with packages and money left over, too! Cause for celebration. And where else to celebrate but at Serendipity, the classy ice cream parlor-boutique.

Before bidding a fond farewell to Bloomingdales, I stopped on the main floor to spray myself with the most expensive perfume from the sample counter. I walked the few blocks toward Serendipity, feeling terrific. Strolling on the East Side always makes me feel good. I love the East Side. Things are so much classier there. No winos in doorways, no Broadway Crazies. Well, if they are crazy, money allows them to be called "eccentric."

Even the people spilling out of office buildings have that crisp air of success. As I crossed the avenue, I noticed a tall, gorgeous woman draped in black chiffon. She was carrying a modeling portfolio under her arm as she hastily hailed a cab. I began thinking of Laura Hunt again, and that whole posh world of making millions. For a moment, I reconsidered that frozen hot chocolate. After all, if I ever seriously considered modeling, I shouldn't be a fat slob. But I weakened and decided to feed my face as planned.

When I reached Serendipity, I chose a corner booth, as always. That way, I could observe everyone else who came in. I loved doing that. I can spend hours watching smartly dressed people sitting around over luncheon or sipping cocktails. Mostly, I like noticing how they're dressed; what fashion choices they've made.

Waiting for my order, I sized up the two women seated near me. Did her embroidered blouse really go with jeans or was it poor planning? Her companion wore western boots and a long paisley skirt. The clothes looked snappy, but her hair wasn't right: too long and frizzy. I checked out the other women seated around, rating them all on a fashion scale of one to ten. No one got more than a seven. Imagining myself in my new outfit, I gave myself an objective nine. Nine and a half, maybe.

When my frozen hot chocolate arrived, I nibbled it slowly, hoping to make it last forever.

It'd been a wonderful day. Absolutely perfect!

That night, I fried up my garlic and onions, ate a dinner of fresh fruit and called my parents. I told them about my wonderful day and what a terrific time I'd had.

Though Mom sounded pleased, I bet she'd rather have had me say I was lonesome. But I wasn't. Not at all.

I was independent at last and loving every minute.

The next three days were perfect. No eating cooked vegetables. No listening to Crissy's wisecracks. I played the phonograph as loud as I liked and watched TV as late as I wanted. I sat for Sarah each morning and my afternoons were free.

One day, I went to the Plaza Hotel, ordered iced tea in the Palm Court and watched the rich checking in and out. I went to a fashion show at Macy's, where free samples of make-up were given out, plus a free face analysis. At Lord & Taylor, I sampled a new cologne being distributed on the main floor. I stood in line four times and got four samples! The weather was wonderful; sunny and not too hot. Perfect for strolling through the city.

On the fourth day, Sarah decided to have a birthday party for her doll, Lavinia.

"She's been naughty again, but I'm going to forgive her."

As a special treat, I took her to Woolworths, where we bought balloons and streamers. Then we stopped at the bakery to pick up some petit fours. We hung the decorations, and the dollies had a great time. So did I.

I told Sarah all about my excursions around the city, and she listened with interest.

"Isn't that grand." She sighed, with perfect British charm. "When I'm big, I shall do that, too."

At last I'd found a kindred spirit. She was only five years old, but we were pals.

"Listen, would you like to come with me tomorrow?" (I'd begun feeling guilty about not taking Sarah out. There was no one in the park for her to play with, and sitting down there was a bore, anyway.)

"Oh, could I?"

When Mrs. Hallifax came home, I checked it out. She insisted that if I took Sarah all day, I get paid by the hour. I didn't argue. Sarah was cute, but I wasn't that charitable!

The next day, Sarah and I went sightseeing. But not to dumb places like the Statue of Liberty and the Empire State Building. Instead, I took her to Madison Avenue. Sarah wore a starched organdy pinafore, shiny patent leather shoes and little socks with lace cuffs. She looked as if she'd stepped right out of a story book. I was glad I'd worn my new Bloomies outfit, so I wouldn't seem like a slob beside her!

As we strolled around, I pointed out the fanciest shops and most exclusive boutiques. We found a shoe store whose window had four-hundred-dollar boots and three-hundred-fifty-dollar satin evening pumps. There was a jewelry shop selling delicately handcrafted bracelets, rings and pendants. We passed a plant store with windows that looked like a jungle: pools of running water, palm trees, ferns, and parrots flying around. Then we noticed a nail salon. From the outside, it looked more like someone's antique living room.

Sarah was suitably impressed. "When I'm older, I shall go inside."

"Why wait," I said, feeling bold. "After all, we look rich and terrific. Let's take a peek."

Inside, the walls were bright red lacquer. There were shelves of golden bamboo and a bar in the corner. Customers were seated under large rice-paper umbrellas, sipping tall cool drinks.

"Another Rum Gardenia for Mrs. Jamison," a salesman called. Then he turned to us. To my surprise, he didn't look at us cross-eyed or ask us to leave. "May I help you?"

"I'm inquiring about your prices," I said, trying to sound at least a little British.

"Certainly." He smiled politely. "We carry only the finest porcelain nails. The fee is forty-five dollars to apply a set of ten."

"Thank you, perhaps I'll return tomorrow."

"And I shall return when I'm older," Sarah added.

Once outside, she started giggling. "That was fun. Let's go to another."

So we did; this time, a ritzy jewelry store specializing in gold and diamonds. There must've been a fortune in jewels sparkling on silk-lined silver trays. Once again, the decor was elegant, and people were seated around, sipping champagne. (I guess all those fancy places have to get people drunk before they'll spend money!)

This time, I pretended I was very British; looking for a gift for my Aunt Lavinia. The salesman showed me several sets of diamond earrings, and I informed him I'd think about it. All the salespeople were so nice, I was beginning to believe I could afford that stuff.

Then it was off to a lovely little store that dealt exclusively in music boxes. There were beautifully intricate ones nestled on every counter. The owner showed us the prize of her collection, an antique music box made in 1875 and valued at twenty thousand dollars. Sarah fell in love with a bisque ballerina who danced to *Swan Lake*.

"Perhaps I'll return. Penelope loves music boxes."

By three o'clock, we realized we were starving. We walked to Fifth Avenue and bought hot dogs from a vendor. Hardly a ritzy lunch, but all I could afford.

Sarah bit into her hot dog, wiping her chin with a napkin. "It's been a grand day, Laura. Thank you."

It'd been fun playing Let's Pretend. The fact that I'd enjoyed the fantasy as much as a five-year-old didn't escape me; but I didn't care.

"Can we do it again?"

"Sure," I said. "Tomorrow."

Chapter 10

That evening I went through my usual ritual: frying up garlic and onions, then calling my folks. I told them I'd made sixteen dollars that day. I'd take Sarah on another "excursion" the next day and make the same. Mom said she was happy, but she didn't sound it. Dad went through the double latching bit again, though I assured him I was perfectly safe.

Why do parents make such a fuss over nothing?

Being independent was easy!

I prepared my dinner of fresh fruits, cold cucumber and carrot sticks, then looked through the newspaper, making lists of possible places to take Sarah the next day. But I'd bring money next time, in case we went someplace affordable.

When I arrived the next morning, Mrs. Hallifax was thrilled to see me.

"Sarah hasn't stopped talking about your delightful day together, Laura. She's in her room dressing now. She insists on looking quite grown-up, just like you. How on earth did you know she'd enjoy shopping? Most five-year-olds loath it. Crissy's a fortunate child to have such a considerate sister."

"Crissy?"

"Why yes. You must delight her all the time, taking her splendid places." She handed me a five dollar bill. "Take this extra money. You girls stop off somewhere and have a lovely lunch."

I felt suddenly guilty. "Listen, Mrs. Hallifax, I didn't do anything. I only took Sarah to places I enjoy going myself."

"So much the better." She smiled. "Then I know you'll *both* have a grand time. I'm auditing a lecture this afternoon, then doing some research at the Columbia library. See you about four?"

She was out the door before I could argue the point.

I went into Sarah's room where she had two crisply starched dresses lying on her bed.

"Which should I wear?" she asked. "The pink or the white?"

"White, I think. Need any help buckling your shoes?"

"No thank you. I'm going to be quite grown-up all day. Where are we going, Laura?"

"Wait and see," I told her. "It's a surprise."

We took the bus to the Pierpont Morgan Library, an old mansion on Madison Avenue. Morgan was a famous railroad tycoon and financier in the nineteenth century. I guess he was like all those barons of industry who robbed people blind, but he sure knew how to live. Originally, he built the place as his private library, but now the building's a public museum, with thousands of rare books, illuminated manuscripts and folios.

A dumb place to take a little kid, right? I'd never been there myself. But there was something I wanted Sarah to see.

Lewis Carroll was freaky about little girls and took pictures of them all the time. One of his little friends, Alice Lidell, was the girl he wrote *Alice in Wonderland* for. Several photos he'd taken of her were on exhibit, and I couldn't wait for Sarah to see the resemblance.

We entered the building, with its marble floors. It was cool and quiet inside, with very few visitors. At the sides of the entrance hall and in the exhibition hall were long wooden cases with glass tops. Inside were yellowed handwritten manuscripts, letters and photographs. Sarah had to stand on tiptoe to see them. She's a polite little kid, so she didn't complain, but I knew she was wondering what the heck we were doing there.

Looking through the cases, I finally found the right one. There were several snapshots of Victorian children, wearing long smocked nighties and fancy dresses. Two were of Alice Lidell; one a profile of her seated in a garden, looking grown-up and pensive.

"See, Sarah," I said, lifting her up. "That's the girl from *Alice in Wonderland*."

She stared in delightful surprise. "Is it really? I think she looks like me!"

"I think so, too. You could be twins."

"I haven't a dress like that," she said, practically, "but Penelope does. Was Alice a famous little girl?"

"Very."

"Then I shall name a dollie for her."

A woman passing by noticed the resemblance, too. "Your sister's lovely. A face from a story book."

"Does that make me famous, too, Laura?"

"I guess so. For today, anyway. Let's pretend you're famous all day today, all right?"

"Oh, could we?" she bubbled. "We'll pretend I live in a mansion."

"This mansion?"

"Yes, that's perfect."

So for nearly an hour, Sarah and I strolled through the rooms of the Morgan mansion, pretending she owned everything. We stopped in the East Room to admire the Persian rugs and walls of books. There must've been thousands of them, from floor to ceiling. There were steps going up to a second level that was filled with old leather-bound volumes in stamped gold bindings. The ceiling was covered with gold leaf and paintings, and a beautiful tapestry hung over the fireplace. In the Rotunda, we sat on a hand-carved bench (one of the few seats where sitting's allowed), and Sarah pretended we were waiting for the butler to bring tea. In the West Room, we admired the red satin wallpaper and red velvet easy chairs. Here the ceiling was hand-carved oak. A huge painting of Pierpont Morgan himself hung over the fireplace.

Sarah frowned. "He looks quite mean. But I'll pretend he's my grandfather."

"How is old Grandad?"

"Quite well, thank you."

A guard tapped me on the shoulder. "Tell the little girl not to walk off the red carpet," he cautioned. "She's gotta stay off the wooden floor."

"Even if I'm famous?" asked Sarah.

"Even so," he grunted.

"You should fire that guy," I whispered. "Shall we stroll through the conservatory, Miss Sarah?"

She giggled. While the guard wasn't watching, Sarah played a fast game of hopscotch on the marbled floor.

"Guess we should leave now," I said. "Cook's making cabbage for lunch. Pretty soon, this whole place'll *stink!*"

Sarah waved goodbye to the guards. "Wait till I tell Lavinia where I've been. She's such a nosy dollie, I have to tell her everything."

"That's my next surprise," I said. "Now we're going to visit Lavinia's cousins!"

We climbed the steps of The Museum of the City of New York, then took the elevator to the second floor. On display there was a huge exhibit of eight hundred dolls from all over the world: an entire roomful of them, posing behind glass panels.

We saw papier mache dolls, china bisque dolls with plump, dreamy faces, a German pegwood doll dressed as a peddlar with tiny combs, scissors, threads and brushes in her lap basket. There were dolls with wax faces and kid leather hands; child dolls from the nineteenth century Paris manufacturer, Jumeau, called bébés, with chubby arms and legs. There were Chinese temple dancers, and figures dressed in Arabian, Indian and African costumes. There were dolls in wedding dresses—even dolls in mourning clothes with long black taffeta dresses and black armbands. We saw clowns, ringmasters, corn husks and acorn dolls. There was a large collection of American dolls, including Kewpies, the Campbell Kids, Mickey Mouse, Betty Boop and the ever-popular Raggedy Ann. We even saw Charlie Chaplin, Cher and The Beatles dolls. There was a whole case of Victorian dolls, too, dressed just like Penelope and Lavinia.

Sarah was delighted. She oohed, aahed, pointed and jumped for joy. I got a kick out of seeing her so excited. She especially liked the Queen Elizabeth doll, dressed in her coronation robes.

"I was in Westminster Abbey once," she said. "But I was just a baby and don't remember it."

Staring at the dolls for ages, she was thrilled to find one that looked like Lavinia. It was wearing a bridal gown and carrying a bouquet of satin flowers.

"Well, I'll have to call mine *Mrs.* Lavinia, now!"

After that, we looked at the collection of dollhouses, then went to the gift shop. Sarah clutched her little straw purse in which she'd stuffed two dollars. But she didn't spent it. Nothing looked quite right. I knew what she really wanted was Mrs. Lavinia to add to her collection!

We had lunch in a little coffee shop on Lexington Avenue, with chocolate mousse for dessert. Then we did some more window shopping. I was beginning to wilt, but Sarah was peppy as ever. She glanced in the stores, then walked down shady side streets lined with brownstones.

Suddenly, she stopped by a building and pointed. "Look, Laura. More of Lavinia's cousins. May we go in?"

I read the picture poster tacked on the entrance:

ANTIQUE CLOTHING, DOLLS, MINIATURES AND COLLECTIBLES

From the Estate of Mrs. Marian Mumfry

AUCTION TODAY 3 P.M.

"This isn't a museum," I explained. "It's an auction gallery. They've lots of old things for sale."

"Lavinia's cousins for sale? Oh may we look, please?"

I'd never been to an auction before, and the lure of antique clothing was overwhelming. "Sure, why not."

We climbed the stairs to a large warehouse-type room. It was filled with tons of things: bisque dolls in cases, boxes of old silk parasols and petticoats, toy cradles and hobby horses. There were shelves of lead soldiers, several dollhouses, an old calliope and racks of clothing. Not Salvation Army stuff, but beautiful dresses from 1890 through the forties.

"Would you like a paddle?" asked the woman at the desk.

"No thank you," said Sarah. "I like dolls."

She smiled. "If you'd like to bid, sign up for a paddle. Only people with paddles may bid at auction time."

"So that's how it works," I said. (I'd seen lots of movies where people at auctions sneezed or scratched their heads and wound up with million dollar urns by mistake.) "How much does a paddle cost?"

"Nothing. Just write down your name and address. The auction begins in a few minutes. There's still time to view the items."

I signed up while Sarah looked for more of Lavinia's relatives. Then, of course, I couldn't resist looking through the racks of clothing.

The dresses were gorgeous: long paisley wools and

silk Victorian gowns with the tiniest waists I'd ever seen. There were slinky satin numbers from the twenties and bugle-beaded capes from the thirties. There were piles of Quaker bonnets, high-buttoned shoes, beaded bags, everything. Needless to say, I was thrilled. What could such wonderful things cost? A fortune, for certain. Just looking through them, feeling the fine fabrics, made me excited.

And then I saw it—without a doubt, the most beautiful dress ever made!

It was a champagne silk afternoon dress from the thirties; yet the very latest "in" fashion. I'd seen something like it in Bloomingdales for $250; but this was much finer. The cut was perfect, with tiny hand stitches around the hem. Across the bodice were delicately appliqued leaves of beige satin in a scallop design, with tiny seed pearls in the center. Tucked inside the hanger was a long silk wraparound shawl, with more seed pearls sewn in a leaf design.

I held it up to me. A perfect fit. Even the length was right. Once in a lifetime, a dress that beautiful comes along. Fit for a movie star. Something Gene Tierney might've worn in *Laura*. Perhaps a famous star *had* worn it!

I was still drooling over it when Sarah tugged at my skirt. "There's a big trunk filled with dollie clothes in the corner. May I look?"

"Sure," I said, not wanting to take my eyes off that dress. If only it were mine! I could see myself in it, sipping tea in the Palm Court, gliding through the lobby of the Plaza, hurrying down the entrance steps into my waiting limousine. It was a magic dress, certain to transform anyone who wore it into a magical person.

"Laura, I found a dress for Lavinia. See that lovely pink one in that trunk. Do you think I might buy it?"

"Buy it?" I laughed. "Sorry Sarah, this stuff's too expensive for us. Besides, that trunk'll be sold as one lot. See that number on the side? That means it's all one item."

"Is it called a lot because there are a lot of things?"

"Maybe." I nodded. "Or because they cost a lot of money."

Just then, the auctioneer pounded his gavel and people began sitting down in the rows of folding chairs. They had their paddles in hand, ready to start bidding.

I took Sarah's hand, and we grabbed two seats up front.

"Maybe we can't bid," I said, "but let's watch and see who does."

"I hope someone nice buys Lavinia's dress." She sighed, watching the trunk being carried up front.

"And I hope someone nice buys *that* dress." I sighed, watching the rack with my dream dress wheeled out in front of me.

The auctioneer began.

"This afternoon, we have many interesting items from the estate of Mrs. Marian Mumfry. As usual, there will be a ten percent commission on each catalogued item. We ask you to pick up your purchases within twenty-four hours. We'll begin with lot seventy-two, a blue tulle evening dress from the thirties."

A young woman assistant took the dress from the rack and held it in front of her for bidders to see. With cool efficiency, the auctioneer glanced around the room, picking up bids as paddles were raised.

"Twenty is bid. We start at twenty. Thirty up front. Forty in the back. Far right at fifty. Still the front row at sixty. Bidder is the far right at seventy. Selling at seventy."

He pounded his gavel, then continued.

"Next is lot forty-three. A paisley wool robe. Opening bid of seventy-five. Seventy-five is bid. At seventy-five. Anyone give more? Eighty-five is bid. At eighty-five now. Anyone give more? Selling at eighty-five to paddle one-hundred-seventy-four.

The assistant lifted up a box with the next items for sale.

"Lot thirty-four. Three Quaker hats. I have an order bid of thirty. Thirty is bid. Were you bidding in the second row? Forty is bid. On my right at forty. Forty in the second row. Far right at fifty. Now it's against you on the left at sixty. On the right at seventy. Selling at seventy. Sold at seventy to paddle forty-six."

"This is fun," Sarah whispered.

I nodded. "It's like tennis, watching those paddles

pop up." The auctioneer was so quick, things were going-going-gone within minutes. Still, I was surprised that such fine old clothing was being sold for so little money.

The auctioneer continued until the entire rack of clothes were purchased. Dream dress was on the rack behind, but it wasn't the next item up for sale.

"We now have lot eighty-four. A leather trunk with parasols, cotton petticoats and several doll items. I have an opening bid of forty. Anyone give more? On the right at fifty. Anyone give more? Selling then at fifty, to paddle thirteen."

Sarah nudged me. "That was the trunk with Lavinia's dress. That nice old lady in the back bought it."

"Too bad," I sympathized.

Sarah looked pensive. "I think I'll speak to her. May I?"

"Sure," I whispered, refusing to take my eyes from dream dress until it'd been sold.

As Sarah moved to the back row, I listened while the auctioneer continued to sell off every dress on the rack. There were only two left; mine and a black velvet evening gown. Some of the clothes went for lots of money, yet others were real bargains. I couldn't understand it. Different strokes, I guess.

That suddenly made me think. I had fifty dollars in my purse. If no one bid against me, I might snatch up "dream dress" myself! My heart pounded faster as I prayed no one else would want it.

Now the black velvet was up for bidding. It started at thirty and sold for one hundred. My heart sank. Dream dress was next. Did I stand a chance?

The auctioneer continued.

"Now we have lot eighty-four. A champagne silk cocktail dress from the forties. We have an order bid for twenty. Twenty is bid."

A woman on my left lifted her paddle.

"I have thirty now. Anyone give forty?"

I gulped and raised my paddle.

"Forty is bid. Anyone give more?"

I held my breath and prayed.

"Forty is bid. Anyone give more? Selling then at forty to paddle sixty-two."

The auctioneer pounded the gavel, finalizing the sale.

I couldn't believe it. *I* was paddle sixty-two. The dress was mine! With ten percent commission, it was still only forty-four dollars. I felt all butterflies inside as I got up and walked to the rack to claim my prize. Then I heard muffled chuckles and saw the auctioneer frown.

"Paddle sixty-two, your purchase will be wrapped momentarily. You may pick it up at the back counter. Bidding continues now with lot eighty-one."

"Excuse me," I mumbled. "I didn't know."

Still in a daze, I stumbled over the chairs, looking for the order counter in the back. A cashier checked my paddle number and the lot number I'd purchased.

"We'll have your purchase in a moment."

I paid for my dream dress, and as I waited for wrapping, Sarah ran up to me.

"Something wonderful's happened, Laura. I spoke to that nice old lady who bought the trunk. She only wanted the parasols and petticoats. So I bought Lavinia's dress from her for two dollars."

"Really?"

"She said I might have it for nothing, but that's not fair." She held the little pink organdy dress up proudly. "Isn't it grand? Lavinia will be thrilled. Oh Laura, now I really do feel like Alice in Wonderland."

"That's great," I said, as the cashier handed me my precious package. "And I feel like Cinderella!"

I think we must've glided home; our heads in the sky, our feet never touching ground.

It'd been the most perfect of all perfect days!

Chapter II

It was a magical dress; I was certain. When I returned home, I laid it out on the bed to stare at it. Then I put it on and viewed myself in Mom's full-length mirror. I looked fantastic—much older and more sophisticated. It may sound crazy, but I truly believed that that dress transformed me in some strange way.

Don't laugh. They say most fairy tales are rooted in fact. Lots of people have written heavy books about their deep, psychological meanings. I'd always thought it all baloney, too, until I saw myself in that dress. Suddenly, I *felt* like Cinderella. I could've danced at a ball, charmed a prince, acquired a kingdom, *anything*.

I spun around to glimpse myself from behind. The dress made a soft rustle of silk against my legs. I wrapped the silk shawl around my shoulders. It felt like cool water.

Forty-four dollars—a small price to pay for such alchemy!

That evening, I didn't watch TV. I lay in bed staring at my dress instead. It took me a long time to get to sleep, too. Maybe I was afraid if I closed my eyes, it'd disappear. But it was still there in the morning, draped across the hanger, waiting to be worn.

Of course, I couldn't wear it just any old place. Since it was Saturday and I wasn't babysitting, I had the whole day for myself. I looked through the paper for the appropriate place to take my new outfit. And I found it. The Metropolitan Museum had an exhibit of Richard Avedon's fashion photography.

I made breakfast, took a shower, then sprayed on my sample cologne. It smelled like fresh spring rain. I applied my new sample lipstick: a pale peachy pink. My beige toe polish complimented my new rope sandals. The smidge of lemon I'd washed in my hair added the proper highlights underneath my new straw hat. I slipped into the dress, feeling its cool silk against my skin. Looking wonderfully fashionable and perfectly put together, I left for the museum.

The show was fabulous, filled with life-sized blow-ups of the world's most famous models, taken by the most famous fashion photographer. Some of the shots from the fifties and sixties were of models working before I was born. But I knew all their names: Dorien Leigh, China Machado, Suzy Parker, Veruschka, Dovima—each with her own brand of class and style.

96

At the peak of their beauty, the camera had captured them forever: strolling down quaint European boulevards, sipping champagne in dark, smoky bistros; while advertising and wearing the most expensive gowns, jewels and furs.

How did they feel about growing old, knowing their youth was recorded forever? Did it make them happy or sad? Maybe getting wrinkled and saggy wasn't so awful when you had pictures to prove you were once beautiful. Besides, lots of them had gone on to become actresses, too: Suzy Parker, Candice Bergen, Twiggy, Margeaux Hemingway, Ali Magraw. Their faces had launched them into two careers.

As I strolled by one of the large glass frames, I caught a reflection of myself. For a moment, I was right inside the picture. I, too, was walking down the Champs Elysees beside Dorien Leigh, looking quite as fashionable in my dream dress as Dorien did in her Dior original. I even shared that look of aloof confidence. The dress had given it to me.

With sudden clarity, I realized that modeling needn't be just a fantasy. It could be real for me, too! If wearing just one beautiful dress had made me feel special, imagine what wearing hundreds of them would do!

Returning to look at the photos again, I decided none of those models looked any better than I could've looked—given proper makeup, lighting and clothing.

All the way home, I kept thinking about it. I didn't

bother getting on the bus. I wanted to be alone with my thoughts a while longer. Walking through Central Park, I was so deep in my dream world, I barely noticed the bicycler come skidding by the narrow path beside me.

"Hey lady, watch out!" he shouted, whizzing by.

He'd almost knocked me down, but I was thrilled. He'd called me lady—not girlie or kid. That really convinced me I looked sophisticated and terrific!

Too bad some famous photographer wasn't passing through the park at that moment. If he were, he'd be certain to snap me. The setting was perfect: the summer sun filtering through the trees, the reservoir in the distance. And me, walking serenely down the long, narrow path. If only a camera *could* capture it.

I held that thought as I continued the walk home. Once outside the park, the potential for fantastic photographs grew even greater . . .

. . . Me, Laura Andrews, cool and calm in champagne silk, walking along the crowded avenues . . .

. . . Me, Laura, stopping at the corner fruit stand; pausing just long enough to select one brilliantly red apple and a perfectly matched bunch of green grapes . . .

. . . Me, not waiting to have them placed in a bag, but carrying them in hand lovingly, as if an offering . . .

. . . Me, strolling down Broadway, then toward Riverside Drive. Ignoring the garbage cans, seeing only the trees in the distance. The trees and, of course, the camera: the all-seeing eye that would record my loveliness forever. It was situated on a tripod at the corner of the Drive, waiting to snap every subtle movement. Waiting to record my face for posterity. A face in the misty light. A laugh that floats on a summer's night . . .

. . . Me, selecting a moist green grape and dropping it slowly into my mouth . . .

. . . Me, laughing softly, like a musical note, while a gentle breeze from the water blows a lock of glistening hair across my sculptured face . . .

. . . And me, stumbling over a lump of wire cables, spilling my grapes onto the street. Me, watching my crimson apple roll down the avenue . . .

. . . And someone shouting, "CUT!"

A face peeping out from behind the camera. A sad, comical face with large horned-rimmed glasses. A familiar face. A *famous* face. The wry little grin was un-mistakable. The face of Woody Allen.

Strange. I'd never shared a fantasy with *him* before. Cary Grant, yes. Paul Newman, of course. Even John Travolta. But Woody Allen, never. He was charming, funny, terribly talented, but much too *short.*

A man came running up the street, carrying a large black posterboard under his arm. He looked very embarrassed.

"Sorry, Woody, she got by me. It's my fault she blew the shot."

Allen nodded nervously, shoving his hands in his pockets. He stared at me. "You're a crazy, right?"

I laughed. I wanted to make it the laugh that floats

99

on a summer's night, but it wasn't. It was only a nervous cackle. I stared at the small figure I'd seen enlarged so often on the movie screen: tweed jacket, sueded elbow patches, V-neck sweater, maroon corduroy slacks, hiking boots. How ordinary for a fantasy.

"You look so real," I whispered. "As if I could reach out and touch you."

And I did.

"I'm right," he nodded, moving aside. "A crazy."

He returned to his position behind the camera, removing his glasses to peer through the lens, then called an assistant who quickly came running.

"Have that girl wait."

Suddenly, I was grabbed by the arm and jostled aside.

"Woody says to wait," said the man threateningly.

At last I realized the truth.

This was no fantasy: *this was real.*

. . . "Woody says to wait" . . . the words kept swimming through my head with all their implications.

I'd just ruined a shot in what was obviously a movie Woody Allen was making, right there on Riverside Drive.

I was still dazed, but I knew enough about moviemaking to realize what that meant. Thousands of dollars *wasted,* that's what! Every second of on-location time costs a fortune. I'd read lots of articles about it. A little snippet of film that only lasts seconds on screen can take weeks of preparation and tons of money.

The assistant was still holding my arm tightly. "I'm sorry," I said weakly.

"Stand by please!" someone shouted. "Block it off. Here we go!"

"Listen," the man whispered, "stand here out of the way. And be quiet, okay?"

I sighed, suddenly realizing the irony of everything. All my life I'd dreamed of watching a movie being made. Now I was smack in the middle of one and couldn't enjoy it. Well, why not? Heck, what could Allen do to me—sue? I'd made an honest mistake. Why should it spoil my big opportunity? Whatever happened, I'd deal with it later. Right now, I'd watch the filming.

Dozens of people were standing around the sidewalk's edge and sitting along the curb. All silent, they were watching with interest. Someone nudged the man beside him and pointed in my direction. I could imagine what he was saying . . . "There's the dodo who messed up the shot." For a moment, I felt like burying my face.

Instead, I began noticing all the things I hadn't seen before. Several trucks were parked along the Drive, out of camera range. Some had sound equipment, others were packed with wire and long metal rods. There were people positioned on every corner, carrying walkie-talkies. They all looked more like Upper West Siders than moviemakers. Most of them were in their twenties, casually dressed in tee shirts and jeans. Not at all what

I'd envisioned. No berets, no jodhpurs, no director's chairs.

In the center of the street was one large camera light on an adjustable stand. Two other smaller lights were set on tripods. And, of course, there was the movie camera, at the corner of the block. Woody Allen was peering through it furtively. After several minutes, he gave a hand signal and an assistant held up a slateboard. He smacked it down with a familiar clack.

"Stand by to roll!" someone shouted. "Roll sound! Background action!"

On that signal, an actor walked from the lobby of the building and strolled down the street.

"Cue the man!" the voice shouted.

Another actor ran from the building, glancing nervously up and down the street.

"Cue the woman!" the voice ordered.

An actress passed by in front of the man.

"Cut!" the voice shouted. "And as soon as it burns in, kill it!"

I was fascinated. "What's that mean?"

"Look, hon," the assistant grumbled. "My job's on the line here. Quiet, okay?"

"Doesn't look like much of a scene," said an onlooker.

"Sure doesn't," another agreed. "I've been watching three hours, and they've redone it nine times. They finally had it right."

"Yeah," someone added, glancing at me. "Until you stumbled along. Now they've gotta start over."

My face turned red, and I felt awful. Maybe Allen *could* sue me. What would Mom and Dad say when I told them? Would Woody drag me to court? Put me in jail? If only I'd watched where I was going. If only I hadn't had my head in the clouds. If only . . .

"Someone's on the frame line!" a voice shouted. "Move 'em back!"

The man with the posterboard held it up in front of the crowd, signaling us to move. As everyone began pushing each other, I wound up in the crunch. A perfect chance to make an escape. Scrunching down, I crawled between some people at the crowd's edge. All I had to do was run across the street into my building and they'd never find me. I'd lock myself in until the film crew had gone. The only trace of me would be the strange headline in Variety next day: WACKO CHICK NIXES ALLEN PIX.

Foiled again! A guy in baggy jeans, carrying a posterboard, stood guard at the curb. He'd seen my every move.

"Didn't Woody want to see you?" he asked suspiciously.

"Woody who?"

"Better wait here. This is the last shot."

And my last chance. There was no escape!

I watched nervously as the camera crew packed up for the day. The large movie light on the adjustable stand was carefully lowered into the truck. Technicians hurried around, loading the equipment. Onlookers began filtering off, nodding and mumbling to themselves. Lots of them looked at me. One woman did more than look; she shouted at me.

"Some people will do anything to get attention!"

Another agreed. "That's the problem with making movies on location. You have to deal with street crazies!"

Twice in the past hour I'd been called a crazy. Crazies wear smelly clothes and carry shopping bags! I'd never looked better in my life. A lot of good it'd done me. Dream dress had led me astray.

I noticed two policemen at the corner. Obviously placed there to keep order and arrest intruders. Any minute, I'd be dragged off to jail!

"Can't we forget this whole thing?" I pleaded.

"Not until we've talked to Woody," he said solemnly.

By now, Allen had left his spot behind the camera and was speaking to an actor. Glancing up the street, he pointed in my direction. The actor nodded blankly. My heart pounded. Were they *both* going to sue me?

Then he called an assistant and pointed in my direction again. All *three* nodded and stared at me. If this kept up, my family'd be bankrupt!

My toes wiggled nervously in my sandals as the assistant proceeded up the street in my direction. His face was deadly serious. I had visions of old Western movies where two gunmen sidle up to one another, ready for the shootout.

"What's your name?" he asked.

For a second, I couldn't remember. Then I considered giving a false one, but drew a blank.

"Laura," I whispered.

"A New Yorker, right?"

"Yes."

"From Manhattan?"

"From across the street."

"An Equity member?"

I stared blankly.

He repeated the question. "Do you belong to the union, Actor's Equity?"

"I don't belong to anything. And I didn't mean any harm. Actually, it was my dress. It's sort of—magic. It makes me do things."

"Your dress made you do it?"

I realized how ridiculous that sounded. "It didn't make me do it, but it made it easy. I mean . . ."

"It made you do that business with the grapes?"

"Business?"

"Right. That Blanche DuBois number. Munching grapes and rolling fruit down the street. Your dress made you do it?"

"Oh no." I laughed. "That was an accident. I had no idea you were making a movie here."

He shrugged his shoulder. "No idea? What about

those cameras and lights? What'd you think they were?"

"I didn't see them, honest. I was being the face in the misty light."

I could see he wasn't making the connection. "You know, the laugh that floats on a summer's night? The train that's passing by, but she's only a dream?"

He finally nodded. "Oh, *that* Laura. Otto Preminger, 1944. You think you're Gene Tierney, is that it?"

"Of course not," I said indignantly. "I'm not crazy. Just a little dazed."

"A little? You were on another planet!"

"But I didn't mean any harm. You aren't going to sue me, are you?"

"Sue you? Who told you that?"

"Isn't that what happens when someone messes up a shot?"

"Not quite. But you'll have to sign a legal form."

I gulped. "A legal form? Must I? My parents aren't rich. In fact, they're not here. And they worry about me a lot. They think I'll get into trouble by myself."

"No kidding!"

"But I haven't," I insisted. "I've been double latching—frying garlic and onions—everything. But I'll have to go back to stinky water if they find this out. Listen, I've earned almost fifty dollars. I guess that's not enough, but . . ."

"Fifty dollars sounds right," he said, nodding to another man. "Give her the form." He stared at me again, then shook his head. "New Yorkers. There's nobody like them."

Before I knew it, a chauffeured car, with Woody Allen in the back seat, pulled up at the corner. Then before I could blink, his assistant got in and they all drove away.

I sighed with relief. "Gosh, he's nice. It costs a fortune to refilm a shot. And he settled for fifty dollars."

The assistant laughed. "Woody doesn't want your money. He's *giving* you fifty dollars."

"Giving me? But why?"

He handed me a slip of paper. "This'll explain it."

I read the form. It was a legal release. With my signature, Allen'd have the right to use whatever film footage I'd accidentally fallen into.

"I can't believe it. This means I'm in a Woody Allen movie!"

"Not quite. When Woody sees the footage, he might edit you out. But this gives him the right to use the shots, should he want to."

"Then I *might* be in his movie?"

"Maybe so. There's a good chance the shot'll stay. Woody thought it was a zany bit."

"I can't believe it. Me, starring in a Woody Allen movie."

He tried calming me down. "Legally, Woody can't use those shots unless you sign that paper. You're a nonprofessional, so we need your legal waiver. Understand?"

"Of course, I'll sign it," I said excitedly. My hand shook so, I could barely write my name.

The assistant took out his wallet and removed five ten dollar bills. "Legally, you've gotta be reimbursed, too. Understand?"

"No." I sighed, glancing at the money. "I don't understand anything. But I think it's all fantastic!"

Chapter 12

I got upstairs, too excited to think clearly. All I wanted was to call my parents and tell them the news.

"Hi Mom, it's Laura. Listen, the most fantastic thing's happened. I bought this magic dress at an auction. Really old. It might have been Gene Tierney's, I don't know. Anyway, it's been my fairy godmother all day. I was walking along when I spilled my grapes and bumped into Woody Allen's camera. He gave me fifty dollars, and he's making me a movie star!"

There was dead silence on the other end, followed by a whispery, "Ohmygod."

"Mom, did you hear me? Some people said I was crazy, but I didn't listen. The dress has seed pearls and a stole, and it turned me into Blanche DuBois."

"OhmyGod!" Mom repeated. "Laura, you must be

hallucinating! What happened? Did you get hold of some drug?"

"What's the matter, Mom? Didn't you hear me? I've seen Woody Allen!"

"It's okay, honey. People see strange things on drugs. We'll drive down and get you right away. We'll have your stomach pumped!"

"Mom, you're not listening," I shouted. "It's been the most fantastic day of my life. I'm walking on air! And all I did was trip!"

She started to cry. "You *are* hallucinating. My poor baby! Kevin, talk to her. I'll find the car keys."

Before I got another word out, Mom was off the phone and Dad was on.

"Laura, what's going on down there? Your mother's hysterical. Are you all right?"

"I'm fine, Dad. Never better."

"Have you been double latching?"

"Of course."

"Have you been taking drugs?"

"Of course not!"

It took another twenty minutes to straighten things out, but it wasn't easy. Mom'd already started up the car's engine and pointed herself toward the Lincoln Tunnel. Dad practically had to drag her back into the house. While he did, I talked to Crissy.

"What kind of mess are you in, Laura? The folks are acting nutty. Mom said you've seen a vision. Have you really gone bats?"

After we all calmed down, I explained what'd happened again. I repeated it three times before they finally understood. Mom *never* understood.

"But what did you *do* in this movie, Laura?"

"Nothing, really. I tripped on the street and dropped my fruit."

"For that you got fifty dollars?"

"Woody *loved* it! He said it was hilarious!"

"Even so, fifty dollars. I don't understand show business!"

I was still bursting to tell someone else my good fortune. But I couldn't risk using the phone again. I was too excited to talk sensibly.

I had it. I'd write someone a letter, describing every glorious detail. Who should I write? *Gloria Goggins*, of course! Once she knew it, the world would know it!

I grabbed several sheets of paper. This'd be a long letter, making up for the ones I hadn't written all summer. Step by step, I recounted each fantastic detail, knowing they'd turn Gloria green with envy. Of course, I omitted the part about tripping on the street. I merely said Woody Allen noticed me walking home and begged me to be in his movie. A tiny lie.

I chuckled to myself. When Gloria received that letter on Fire Island, her bumbling beach boys and sappy parties would seem like kids' stuff. I stamped it, opened the back door and dropped it down the mail chute. My only regret was not being there when she opened it. Gloria always looked ghastly in green!

It'd been a few days since my fateful meeting with Woody Allen, but I still hadn't recovered. Visions of champagne and stardom still danced in my head. Of course, I left some time for the practical aspects of life: food shopping and babysitting for Sarah.

One day when I went to her house, she'd arranged a treat for me. Sarah and her dollies were giving a tea party in my honor. Lavinia wore her auction dress and Mrs. Hallifax had bought jam tarts and macaroons.

"Lavinia and I aren't at all surprised," said Sarah happily. "We *always* thought you looked like a movie star."

What a great kid. You'd never catch Crissy saying a sweet thing like that!

But thoughts of Crissy and my parents were far from my mind. I called each evening, so they wouldn't bug me. But I had more important things to think about. I was reading *Variety* now, and all the other show business papers. I hoped to find some small article about Allen's brilliant new discovery, but never did. Oh well, I'd wait until the film premiered, then get my rave reviews.

At night, I'd watch all the great old movies on TV; the ones dripping with romance and beautiful costumes. The following day, I'd get all the trade papers and read through them again.

But time was running out. Pretty soon, my two week's babysitting would be over. Mrs. Hallifax would finish her course at Columbia, then take Sarah to Florida to visit her sister.

Well, if I had to go back to Windham, at least I'd return a star!

Then came Friday. Fateful, fickle Friday! It wasn't a Friday the thirteenth, but it should've been. It heralded the beginning of heartache, sorrow and despair.

But it started off pleasantly enough. My last day to sit for Sarah, I took her to a Broadway gift shop to buy a present for her aunt. She selected a pretty glass tray, and we brought it home to wrap.

"I'll write you when I'm on vacation," she said. "Mother writes it down, but I tell her the words."

"I'll write, too," I promised. "We've had fun, haven't we?"

"Yes, Laura, it's been super!"

I helped Sarah pack her suitcase for the plane. When Mrs. Hallifax returned, she thanked me again for the wonderful times I'd given her daughter. Again, she went on about how fortunate Crissy was; and again, I felt guilty. (Well maybe if someone paid me two dollars an hour to live with Crissy, I'd be nice to her, too!)

I said my farewells, then picked up the mail. There was an answer from Gloria Goggins and I couldn't wait to read it:

Dear Laura,

News from you, at last. I know you're an awful letter writer, but you really should make some effort.

I was amazed to hear of your accidental good fortune. It was an accident, wasn't it? Imagine, being in a movie. Is it a comedy? It must be, if Woody Allen's making it. I guess you were wearing some funny outfit, right?

My dad says you shouldn't get too excited about it, though. Lots of film winds up on the cutting room floor. The stupid parts are the first to go. But at least you had one fun day. Things must've been pretty boring in the Catskills, eh? Why else would you want to be stuck all alone in the sticky city!

If you get too terribly desperate, you can always take the train out here. There are so many gorgeous guys, I've stopped counting. Boys, boys, boys, as far as the eye can see. I might even be able to fix you up with someone.

Got to run now. There's a funtastic volley ball game cooking on the beach.

Tatafornow,

Gloria

P.S. If you come out, take a sunlamp treatment first. Your pasty white skin'll stand out on the beach like a popsickle stick!

What nerve! I might've known Gloria'd be too jealous to congratulate me. But as long as she spread the word, who cared!

I fried up my garlic and onions, then stretched out with my theatrical papers. I read them faithfully from cover to cover and was beginning to learn a lot about the movie business. There was a fascinating article about making TV commercials and another about one producer suing another.

Then I saw it. A little item on the bottom of page 17:

ALLEN PIX WOES

Woody Allen's new movie has been plagued with problems since production began last month. The star scheduled to play the lead broke an ankle while skiing. Now, all exterior footage has been scrapped while Allen does major rewrites. Funny business ain't so funny, is it, Woody?

All exterior footage has been scrapped . . . those six words popped from the page, with all their awful implications. I was exterior footage. That meant I'd been scrapped, too! My bright, shining career had just been smashed to a thousand pieces!

At first, I refused to believe it. I reread that rotten article six times. Then I got mad. I called the office of *Variety*, demanding to know who'd printed such a crappy item. They hung up on me several times, but I kept calling. I had to be certain it was true! Finally, I got hold of a guy in charge of that department. I demanded to know where he got his information.

"From the horse's mouth, of course. I had coffee with Woody last night. He scrapped the whole story."

"But why? I happen to be in the business myself and know it's a great movie. With a great new star. Her footage is hilarious!"

"That's the trouble. Woody wants to be considered a serious filmmaker, not just a laugh machine."

"That's stupid."

"Maybe so. But it's in the dumper, lady!"

I hung up.

I'd like to say that I then became philosophical. After all, life has its ups and downs, and everyone learns to roll with the punches, right?

Wrong.

I felt like screaming, tearing my hair.

What's worse, it was only the beginning of my downhill road to shame and humiliation!

116

It didn't take me long to realize I'd lie, cheat, steal, *anything* to get back in that movie. Something weird had come over me, and I'd become a nut. A *depressed* nut.

I refused to wind up on the cutting room floor!

I wandered around the house that evening, unable to do anything. I hadn't been to the store, so there wasn't any food; only fried onions and garlic. How I managed to sound normal when Mom called, I don't know. Guess we have inner resources. Anyway, as soon as I hung up, I schlumped back into my depression and stayed there. Two days. Don't ask what I ate; I didn't. Don't ask who I saw; I didn't.

But by the end of the second day, I'd formulated a plan.

I'd find out everything there was to know about Woody Allen.

And when I had, I'd make him put me back in his movie!

When Mom called that evening, I lied.

It was the first of many lies.

"Laura, we can't wait to see you. What bus are you taking tomorrow?"

"I'm not, Mom. I can't come up yet."

"What do you mean? Why not?"

"Mrs. Hallifax wants me to stay another week. She's taking some morning seminars and needs me to sit for Sarah. She's got no one else to do it, and I promised!"

Now I was really alone. With Mrs. Hallifax gone, the building was truly deserted. I saw no one but the doorman, and he was always napping. Good thing I had Woody's money because I started living on it. I couldn't afford fresh fruits and vegetables any more, so I stocked up on peanut butter and crackers. I didn't bother making the bed or doing dishes any more.

Believe me, I was a mess!

Chapter 13

Where does a person go to find out about Woody Allen?

What are his hobbies? His favorite restaurants? Where does he live?

I couldn't hope to change his mind until I'd met him. But how was I to do that?

I began at the library downtown, looking through back issues of magazines. I found feature articles in *Time*, *Newsweek* and the *Sunday Times*, plus tons of reviews of past movies.

All the articles agreed. Allen was a quiet, introverted man who shunned crowds. He was born in Brooklyn and now lived in a Fifth Avenue penthouse. He was very shy and had only a few close friends, including his favorite co-stars, Diane Keaton and Tony Roberts. He rarely walked on the street alone, afraid people might stop him. When he did venture out, he often wore disguises to fend off fans or popped into his chauffeured limousine. His only real haunts were an East Side restaurant and a pub where he played clarinet once a week.

Not exactly a social butterfly, right? And not a lot to go on, but a start.

I decided to begin with Elaine's, Woody's favorite restaurant.

First, I phoned and left a message, hoping he'd call me back. I pretended I was Diane Keaton. I was told he wasn't there. I called again. This time, I changed my voice and pretended I was Tony Roberts. He still wasn't there. On the third phone call an hour later, I changed my approach. I said I was an old school chum from Brooklyn who'd just been hit by a car and was bleeding to death in a pay phone.

The voice on the other end was unimpressed. "Sorry, Mr. Allen isn't here."

Clearly, I was being given the runaround.

Okay, if Woody Allen wouldn't accept phone calls, I'd go to Elaine's in person. I hadn't eaten all day anyway.

From my research, I knew Elaine's was a trendy place for the literary and show biz set. And hard to get into during dinner hours. I decided to look my best. I put on my Bloomies outfit and my large straw hat. I stuffed some money in my purse and took a bus to the East Side.

Elaine's didn't look like much outside: just an ordinary Italian restaurant. I walked through the door and glanced around. It was eight thirty, and the dinner crowd had already arrived. There was only one table available in the front dining room. I walked toward it, but didn't get far.

A waiter approached me. "Sorry, no tables."

He signaled another waiter, who opened the front door.

"That's all right, I'll wait."

"No tables all night," he said.

Then I noticed he was getting signals from a woman seated by the bar, checking through a pile of receipts. She was middle-aged, mean looking, with dark hair and glasses. Elaine Kaufman, obviously. My research was paying off. I knew if Elaine didn't like someone's looks, she was apt to throw them in the street. But somehow, I sensed that that empty table was awaiting Woody Allen, and I wasn't about to be heaved out.

"That's all right." I smiled. "I'll sit at the bar."

The waiter gave me a serious glance, trying to judge if I was old enough to drink. I looked aloof. Elaine gave him the nod. I'd passed inspection.

Taking a seat at the bar, I acted casual, pretending I'd ordered drinks tons of times. (Actually, I'd never tasted anything but wine, and that had made me sick!)

"Yes, Miss?" the bartender asked.

I thought of something gay and romantic. "Brandy Alexander, please."

He shook his head and frowned. "We don't make them."

The only other drink I'd heard of was a Screwdriver, so I ordered it. He brought me a tall orange drink, and I sipped it. It tasted bitter, but at least the juice had Vitamin C.

I glanced around, noticing the checkered tablecloths and walls filled with theater and film posters. Someone at a corner table looked familiar: a woman with a big feathered hat and lots of makeup. An actress, I supposed. Three men with elbow-patched jackets and serious expressions sat in heated conversation. Writers, no doubt.

Elaine put down her receipts and glanced around the room, too. She looked like a presidential Secret Service guard with X-ray vision and eyes behind her back. She threw me a questioning glance. I sipped my drink faster and pulled my straw hat down further, attempting to look foreign and mysterious. Slowly, she left her seat and walked in my direction. Would I get the old heave-ho? No, she stopped to grab a waiter's arm.

"There are five people at table three. I've only got four dinner receipts. That guy orders a main course or gets out!"

The waiter nodded nervously.

"And make them order more wine!" It was a voice everyone could hear. Elaine didn't care. This was her place, and things went her way. Eat and drink or get out!

She glared at me again as I gulped down the rest of my drink. Hoping to prove I was a good customer, I ordered another.

Halfway through the second Screwdriver, the room began spinning. The faces at the bar began turning into fuzzy blobs. The smells of Italian sauces and vinegar salads stopped making me hungry and began making me sick.

And I felt as if I was slipping off the bar stool!

I looked down at myself to check. I was still there. It must've been the room that was slipping away.

"Are you all right?" asked the person beside me. He was a tall man with a Pinnochio nose, who smelled of clam sauce. Or did he look like clam sauce?

"Perfectly," I said, refocusing my eyes. "Another drink, bartender."

I knew if I didn't keep ordering, Elaine would have me booted out. So I kept ordering. And drinking!

Soon, I couldn't distinguish Elaine's face from all the other blurry ones floating past me. The woman in the feathered hat now had three eyes. The man at the front table was wearing his tie in his mouth. The fat man across the room had turned into Oliver Hardy. And the little guy with glasses and an Army jacket looked just like Woody Allen.

I blinked.

It was Woody Allen!

He must've come in without my noticing. (An Army band could've come in without my noticing!)

Stumbling off the stool, I began weaving toward his table. This wasn't easy. All the tables floated in front of me, and my feet were stuck in glue. I'd almost reached Woody when a waiter grabbed me by the arm. Good thing he did, because I was falling down.

"May I help you?"

"Why yes," I said, pushing the words past fuzzy cotton. "I've gotta talk to Woody—I mean Misserallen—I mean, *him*."

I leaned toward the floating tables. Woody Allen, his spaghetti, meat balls and the waiter all merged into one.

"You'd better leave now," the waiter snapped, grasping my arm harder. "Don't disturb our guests."

My stomach rolled over and I knew I was going to throw up.

"Where's the bathroom?" I asked, feeling myself turn green.

He pointed me in the right direction. I made it inside just in time.

My head still hanging over the sink, I heard Elaine's voice outside the door.

"Where'd that wacko go?" she yelled.

"In the ladies room. She looked lousy,"

"When she comes out, she pays up and leaves. I thinks she's a deadbeat."

I'd been given the axe! No chance to talk to Woody now. Elaine was on the other side of the door, waiting to pounce! All the stories I'd read about her were true. She protected her favorite customers like a guard dog and bit into those she didn't like.

But I *had* to talk to Allen. Should I shove a message in his meatballs? Not a bad idea. I'd write a note and sneak it to him. My head still throbbing, my eyes blurry, I took a pad and pencil from my purse. I managed to scratch out a few lines. But they didn't make much sense:

Dear Mr. Allen,
I'm desperate. You hold my future in your hands. I'll be waiting outside. I hope you know me, even though I have no grapes and apples. Still, I think I deserve to be a star.
                    Laura, (from your dumper movie)

I washed my face and looked at myself in the mirror. Death warmed over! But if I got the note to Woody, it'd all be worth it.

I pushed open the ladies room door. As I'd expected, Elaine was standing on the other side, her arms clenched across her chest.

"You've got a bar bill," she said sternly. "Pay it."

"Naturally," I said, wobbling through the door.

From the corner of my bloodshot eyes, I spied Allen's table. (Thank God it'd stopped spinning around.) Halfway through his spaghetti dinner, he was glancing through a book. Most of his face was buried under a baggy hat. One sneakered foot protruded from under the table.

Passing by, I accidentally on purpose tripped over that foot. He pulled back nervously and hid his face with his hand. (You'd think the guy was Phantom of the Opera, the way he hated to be seen!) Still, it'd given me enough time to lean over and drop the note in an ashtray. Luckily, Elaine didn't see this. Neither did Woody; he was too busy hiding. But he'd find it soon enough.

As for Elaine, my clumsiness had been the last straw. "Pay up and leave," she ordered, handing me my bill. "Drunks are a pain, but young drunks are the worst!"

I tried thinking of a super sarcastic reply. All my brain could manage was, "Oh yeah?"

Then I stared at the receipt. Seven dollars and fifty cents! It seemed unfair to pay a fortune for three wretched drinks I'd upchucked in the bathroom! But I had no choice. I parted with my money and left with as much dignity as I could muster.

I only stumbled once more before reaching the door.

I must've hung around that street for over an hour. Woody never showed. I peeked through the windows, but couldn't see anything past the curtains. It was almost eleven o'clock. Had Woody read my note? I hoped it didn't sound too wacky. Maybe he'd escaped over a rooftop! But I couldn't go back inside to check.

Eleven thirty

I was scared to go home alone much later. Either Allen had slipped out a side entrance or fallen asleep. Which is what I wanted to do, too.

I had enough money left for a cab, so I took one home.

When I got upstairs, my stomach turned over again. It felt as if it had been stretched from one end of the room to the other. I spent most of the night in the bathroom.

And for what? *Nothing.*

The whole evening had been a very expensive waste of time!

Chapter 14

I had disgusting dreams when I did get to bed. Woody Allen was stirring me up in a giant vat of spaghetti, while singing, "Laura is the face in the meatball sauce."

I didn't wake up until noon. When I did, my head pounded and my stomach grumbled. But I couldn't eat. There was nothing but peanut butter, the thought of which made me want to vomit again.

I crawled into a cold shower, but left the bathroom door open, hoping Woody Allen might call. Of course, when my head cleared, I realized I hadn't written my phone number on that idiotic note. He probably never read it, anyway.

I went back to bed and stayed there all day, planning my next move.

Luckily, it was the night Allen played clarinet at

Michael's Pub, and I was determined to snare him in that jazz den. Checking through my research notes, I learned he usually did one or two sets with the combo, starting at nine o'clock. I'd get there at eight thirty.

But what should I wear? He probably hadn't noticed me at Elaine's, even though I'd fallen into his food. I'd wear dream dress. That would make him remember. It would bring me good luck, too. And my big straw hat and rope sandals. I put twenty-five dollars in my purse; more than enough for dinner.

I took the bus to Second Avenue, enjoying the lovely cool evening. The hint of rain helped clear my remaining cobwebs.

I'd never been in Michael's Pub; a really pretty place. It had frosted glass doors, English Tudor decor, dark wood paneling and large globed chandeliers. The headwaiter greeted me at the entrance.

I craned my neck to see into the small dining area. It was already roped off and filled. "I'd like a table for dinner."

"Sorry. Reservations only," he said, gesturing toward the bar on the right.

Oh well, I'd order a drink (a soda, this time!). A table would probably open up soon.

But walking into the bar, my mouth fell open. It was a tiny room, so crowded the counter was barely visible. Dozens of people stood around, their drinks up near their noses, they were so crunched together.

Was this the "singles scene"—everyone waiting to hit on someone? I checked my watch. Eight forty-five. I hoped they'd all pair off before the music started.

Hah!

It didn't take me long to realize that everyone had come for the same reason I had. To see Woody Allen. To get a glimpse of him. And there were at least fifty people in front of me! Shoving my way back around the partition, I gestured to the headwaiter.

"I have to get into the dining room. Aunt Lavinia's at that corner table."

"Sorry." He smiled.

"You don't understand. Her apartment's burning down, and her French poodle's inside!"

He nodded politely. "Reservations only."

"You'd let a little dog die? I've never heard of such a thing!"

"*I* have, Miss. I've heard them all. When Woody plays here, we hear lots of stories: fires, floods, you name it. Sorry. Reservations only. Have a drink at the bar, if you like."

I stamped back into the bar. If possible, it was more crowded. Sardine time! It was such a tight squeeze, I had no room for my hat. I had to take it off and press it against my chest.

As tall as I am, I couldn't see a thing above the mobs of heads in front of me. The band started up, and everyone pushed closer to the rope partition. Of course, I couldn't see *them*, either. The room divider separating the bar from the dining room hid their faces.

Was Wood Allen in there? Who knew!

"Can you see him?" someone asked.

"I see him," a voice shouted. "A piece of him, anyway. That's his elbow on the right."

There was lots more pushing and jostling while everyone tried for a better position. Someone behind me jabbed an elbow in my ribs. The woman next to me spilled some drink down my dress. So much for my fancy outfit. I should have worn combat boots!

After poking and shoving people, I did finally manage to improve my position. Now, there were only fifteen heads in front of mine. In the inch of space between their necks, I could almost see into the dining room. I thought I spied Allen in the corner. All the other musicians wore black suits and ties, but this one short, skinny guy was wearing faded denim. Most of his face was blurred behind his clarinet, oblivious of the circus taking place by the outer bar.

"Take my spot," a woman offered her friend. "You're leaving for Omaha tonight. You've got to see him before you go."

"I saw him!" someone shouted triumphantly. "That's his reflection in the mirror!"

"Oh, let me see him, too," a woman pleaded. "My babysitter's charging me a fortune!"

A circus. I'm not kidding!

And people were still piling in—from Outer Mongolia, no doubt. You'd think there was a poster hung outside . . . SEE WOODY ALLEN, BUT DON'T FEED THE ANIMALS.

I couldn't figure it. After all, he's so *short*.

"Isn't he fantastic." The woman sighed. "I saw *Annie Hall* seven times."

"That's Woody's head over there, behind the tuba player!"

"I'm not leaving him till I see him. This beer cost me three bucks!"

By now, people were stomping on my feet, and my hat had been trampled in the crunch. I felt the drink drying down the front of my dress, but couldn't bend over to see the damage. I thought of screaming FIRE, to clear the place out, but no one would have heard it.

By the end of the first set, I'd progressed to the crowd's third row. The waiters continued bustling around, and Woody and the band resumed their mellow jazz numbers, while the diners listened calmly and politely.

Meanwhile, back at the bar, we stood scrunched like cattle, popping our eyes and craning our necks.

No one would leave. Seeing an elbow, an earlobe, half a pair of glasses, was better than nothing. Something to tell the folks back home. Sophisticated New Yorkers? Forget it! We were all a bunch of monkeys in a zoo. And I was the biggest chimp of all.

I was too upset to enjoy the music, which was good. Too depressed to care about my dress, which was probably blotchy.

Disgusted and defeated, I finally pushed my way back through the crowd. Some other crazed fan happily took over my tiny space beside the roped partition. Pushing open the door, I noticed dozens more people lined up in the street, waiting for the privilege of being part of the stampede inside.

Were they *all* victims of Woody Allen's scene cuts?

It wasn't fair! I was no goggling tourist from Omaha. I shouldn't be lumped in with these groupies and starry-eyed housewives. I was a star myself. Or should be.

But who was I kidding? I hadn't a chance of *seeing* Allen, never mind meeting him.

Standing there on the sidewalk, a light evening rain falling against my face, I realized I was just another tiny cog in the big wheel of fortune.

But I refused to give up. Somehow, someway, the name Laura Andrews would become a household word!

I got on the bus for home, determined to redesign my Master Plan.

Chapter 15

"There's just as good fish in the sea as ever came out of it." As I lay in bed that night, I kept thinking of that old saying.

It was true. Why should a person with my obvious fame potential hitch her wagon to one star? A short, skinny one, at that. If, by accident, I'd fallen into a Woody Allen movie, just think what I could do by design!

The next morning, I dragged out all the show business papers and began pouring through them again. After all, Woody Allen wasn't the only moviemaker in town. If I played my cards right, I might wind up in a Steven Speilberg or Frances Ford Coppola epic. *Annie Hall* was just one of the movies that had been shot in New York. There'd also been *The Godfather*, *The Marathon Man*, *The Goodbye Girl* . . .

Rereading the papers convinced me I was right. According to *Variety*, the city was crawling with cameras and directors, all making major productions. Suddenly, New York had become Tinsel City's biggest back lot. There was a disco movie shooting in Greenwich Village, a thriller being filmed in Brooklyn Heights and another doing night shooting on the Upper West Side. Since this was right in my back yard, it seemed the best bet. I read the short article:

Riverside residents can't get much sleep these nights. They're complaining about the high-intensity lights set up around the Boat Basin, where the flick *Night Flyers* is in production. Forget it, Upper West Siders. The Mayor knows bit movie productions mean big bucks in revenue. That's show biz!

The Boat Basin! I knew the area well. It was just a mile from home, and I often hung around there. Sometimes after school, Gloria Goggins and I'd bike down to the dock, pretending one of the yachts moored in the Hudson was ours.

It was a lovely section with flagstone steps, stone arches and a large circular fountain. Very romantic. Any movie made there was sure to be a winner. During summer nights, yachts light up the harbor, and the skyline of New Jersey reflects along the river. And the title *Night Flyers* sounded like a mysteriously romantic story.

I'd be perfect for it! I'd wear Dream Dress, stroll along the river by moonlight and be discovered! Re-discovered.

I was all set to go out that night, but Dream Dress wasn't. It had suffered major damages at Michael's Pub and needed a cleaning. I spent the afternoon carefully scrubbing off the liquor stains with a toothbrush and soapsuds.

My lovely straw hat had been demolished, but I didn't care. Without it, the director of *Night Flyers* would get a better look at my face.

I was my old self again, and so excited I could hardly wait. After all, I hadn't thoroughly enjoyed being discovered the first time. But now, I could savor each moment and plan my moves. No stumbling or tripping this time. A romantic movie location required a look of mystery and aloofness. So, standing by the full-length mirror, I practiced my walk. Then I dragged out the step stool and practiced gliding down the flagstone steps. Not bad. If *I* were a famous director, *I'd* notice me.

It would be dark by the river, so I'd need extra makeup. And high heels, not sandals. I rummaged through my closet, looking for an appropriate pair, but had none. Then I remembered Mom's beige silk heels she'd bought in a fit of madness. They were almost new, and only two sizes too small. If I kept my toes scrunched up, I'd manage. The heels were awfully high, which made me look about six feet tall, but that only added to my glamour. I sprayed some perfume on my fan, applied an extra thick layer of mascara, then sat by the window, waiting for night to fall.

I checked the weather report on the radio. Not only would there be a full moon, but it was the August moon, the brightest of the year. The signs were looking good. With any luck, I'd be a star by morning!

As much as I love the city, it always seems strange on a summer night. Unless it's really scorching hot, the streets along Riverside Drive are empty. That night was no exception. Even the Riverside bus was empty, except for a handful of people. An old man in a corner seat stared at me all the way to Seventy-ninth Street, which made me wonder if I'd shoveled on too much mascara. I checked my pocket mirror. Well, it was a bit heavy, but very dramatic. I rubbed some extra rose blusher on my cheeks.

Getting off the bus, I walked the long winding path that leads through Riverside Park toward the tunnel that opens onto the fountain area: the entrance to the Boat Basin. Strolling along, I kept checking for the high-intensity movie lights, but the place seemed totally deserted. No trucks, cameras; nothing. It was so quiet, I could hear a leaf fall. Guess I was too early. I used the extra time to practice walking up and down the flagstone steps in my high heels. After a few turns, my shoes began to hurt, so I took them off and gave my toes a wiggle.

Still no sign of any lights—camera—action, so I sat on the steps and watched the few small boats remaining in the water. They bobbed around by their moorings, licking the water. Even they had no lights.

Where was everyone? I'd envisaged some famous actor dressed in a trench coat, leaning against the lamppost. Where was the mysterious woman in black, dropping a secret message into the river? Where was my big break?

The park seemed deader than a graveyard. Was I the only one there? Suddenly, the implication was obvious. At that moment, I wasn't a potential candidate for stardom, but a potential mugging victim!

Quickly squeezing back into my shoes, I hurried down the steps toward the path that extends along the river. By now the sky was black. The full moon was so brilliant, it cast my shadow in front of me along the walk. That gave me a strangely eerie feeling, as if I were being followed.

Then in the distance, I noticed another person: a woman, walking several yards ahead of me. Thank goodness I wasn't alone. I hurried along, trying to catch up to her. But that wasn't easy in my pinchy shoes. My feet hurt so much, I could only hobble, so I stopped to remove my heels. When I looked up again, the woman was gone.

Now I was definitely alone and getting scared. I'd already walked halfway up the path and knew there wasn't another exit for several blocks. If someone pounced on me from a bush or something I'd have no way of escape. Remembering the karate classes I'd taken when I was twelve, I tried recalling the basic moves, but I'd forgotten them all.

Then I saw it: two faint lights at the end of the path. At least I thought they were lights. Looking closer, I could see they were moving toward me. Two lights, suspended in midair, with hideous faces behind them.

I stopped short and blinked. It wasn't my imagination. Two horribly painted, lit-up faces had come out of nowhere and were careening toward me with flying-saucer speed. Creatures from another planet? I heard the whirl of wheels getting louder as they approached.

Feeling like a trapped rat, I thought of climbing the railing and jumping into the river. But the jagged rocks by the shore would probably have killed me. If they didn't, the polluted water surely would.

As the faces came closer, I could see they were two men on roller skates, wearing punk outfits and baseball hard hats. They were painted with garish red and black horror makeup. The flashlights they'd shoved beneath their chins made them look even more terrifying.

I cringed against the railing, breathless, as they coasted toward me. Now there was one on either side, grinning hysterically. They flashed their lights in my eyes, almost blinding me. Letting out a scream, I threw my purse and shoes in their faces. Luckily, I had the element of surprise. They dropped their flashlights, lost their footing on the skates and fell to the ground.

Then suddenly, a police car came whizzing down the path and I ran toward it, desperately pounding on the window. The policeman flung open the door and stepped out. He, too, was wearing the same horrible fright makeup! He lunged for me, grabbed my shoulder and pulled off my shawl. I screamed again, this time louder than I thought humanly possible. Then I threw my perfumed fan (the only weapon I had left) into his face.

He sneezed and rubbed his eyes. "What's going on?" he yelled back to the other guys, picking themselves up from the ground. "Who is this nut?"

Another cop, with a bright orange crew cut and a safety pin through his nose, jumped from the car. "I didn't get this change," he shouted indignantly, then stared at me. "Hey, this isn't Gloria. What a mess-up!"

"You're telling me," groaned the guy on roller skates. "I think I broke my ankle."

As I ran away from the one crazed cop, the other clamped his hand on my wrist. "No you don't," he said threateningly. "We've got trouble here."

Within seconds, another police car drove by and pulled up in front of the first. Another cop got out. But he looked normal and wore a regular uniform. Then a short, fat man, chewing a cigar, burst from the back seat of the patrol car, shouting hysterically.

"What the heck's going on? Where's Gloria?"

"We must've got our signals crossed," said the guy on roller skates. "I guess she passed us. Then this nutty kid threw *shoes* at me. I'm calling Equity in the morning. My contract doesn't call for injuries!"

Slowly, a large black cloud floated across the full moon. The man spit out his cigar and began pulling his hair. "There goes our natural lighting," he moaned. "I'm another day over budget. I never should've signed for this clinker movie!"

Suddenly, everything began making sense. The fat guy must be the director of *Night Flyers* and all these painted creeps were *actors*.

"Then this isn't *real?*" I asked, half-excited, half-relieved. "It's only a shot?"

"It *was* a shot," snapped the painted policeman, "until you botched it."

"What're you doing here?" asked the real policeman suspiciously.

"It's all right," I assured him. "I'm trying to break into the business."

He nodded knowingly. "That's no business for you, kid. Why not go home, wash your face and be a good little girl."

"Not *that* business," I said, shocked. "*Show* business!"

"It's broken, I know it," mumbled the guy on

roller skates, hobbling over to the police car and climbing in. "My ankle's swelling like a balloon. Geez, I've an audition for a sit-com in the morning. I'll have to cancel."

"You promised police supervision," the director shouted. "Is this how the city treats a major production company?"

"We do our best." The cop sighed. "But we can't control all the crazies."

With the policeman, the fat man and the guy on roller skates staring at me, I realized I was rapidly earning a reputation as a famous West Side wacko.

But it wasn't my fault. It had all been an unfortunate mistake.

Pretty soon, more actors with garish punk makeup began popping out from behind bushes, technicians came in with hand-held cameras, and sound men appeared. Then Gloria, for whom I'd been mistaken. She was the woman who'd been walking ahead of me through the park. They stood around, demanding to know who'd messed up the shot. The fat man pointed his accusing finger.

"It's not my fault," I insisted. "When these creeps came toward me, I thought they were muggers, not actors. Besides, I thought *Night Flyers* was a *love story*."

"For your information," the director boiled. "*Night Flyers* is a horror story about weirdos taking over and terrorizing New Yorkers. But I don't have to tell you about weirdos."

"She's only a kid," said the cop, taking pity on me. "Let's forget it."

"Tell the moon to forget it," the director shouted. "That cloud cover's going to last all night. We'll have to drag out the floodlights, call the lighting technicians back, scrap this footage . . ."

I was on the cutting room floor for the second time. Too late to ask for a bit part now. By morning, my face would be plastered on every director's desk with the caption: DANGEROUS, PROCEED WITH CAUTION!

"Over budget," he kept repeating. "I've gotta call the Coast again. I never should've left Walt Disney!"

"It's your own fault," I said indignantly. "You should've posted signs. You didn't even shout, 'Quiet on the set.' Very unprofessional. I don't think I want to be in your creepy movie, anyway."

"Be in it?" he gasped. "I wouldn't let you buy a ticket to see it! You're insane. This whole town's insane."

By now, the entire cast and crew were mumbling and grumbling. The phony cop I'd thrown my fan at couldn't stop sneezing, insisting he was allergic to perfume. The actor on roller skates was threatening to sue the production company, the Parks Department and the entire city of New York.

"You'd better come with me," said the policeman. "You've caused enough trouble."

"Please don't arrest me," I begged. "It wasn't my fault. I didn't know . . ."

"Relax," he said. "I've got teenagers myself. They never know. Live around here? I'll take you home in the patrol car."

I didn't much like having my beautifully planned evening end up with me in a police car. But looking at those angry faces, it seemed a good idea.

"Just a few blocks from here," I said, climbing into the back seat.

As the policeman turned on the headlights, I took one last look at those horribly painted faces, then bid a sad farewell to my second crack at movie stardom. Driving home, I suddenly realized I had no shoes or purse. I'd lost my fan and shawl, and my dress had gotten ripped in the scuffle.

"My name's Reagan," said the officer, glancing in the rearview mirror. "What's yours?"

"Laura Andrews."

"Your folks know what you're up to tonight, Laura?"

"No, they're hopeless alcoholics."

"Gee, that's rough."

"Yeah well, I'm used to it." I sighed as he turned down West End Avenue. "You can let me off here."

"Nothing doing. I'll see you to your door."

Officer Reagan escorted me into the lobby. Larry the doorman was asleep as usual, and I had to bang until he let us in. Rubbing his eyes, Larry went to the basement and got my spare apartment key. He handed it to me with a sneaky grin.

"You must've had some night."

"None of your business."

"Bet it's not over yet." He yawned.

"What did he mean? Next to Gloria Goggins, Larry was the biggest blab in town. No telling what twisted story he'd be telling by morning: Laura Andrews, dragged home barefoot by the fuzz!

Officer Reagan followed me up in the elevator and waited while I opened the door. I wished I hadn't told him my parents were drunkards because he'd suddenly grown very protective.

"I'll be all right now," I insisted.

But I was wrong. Pushing open the door, I stared straight into the face of my father.

"Laura!" he shouted, looking drained, drooped and rumpled. "Where've you been?"

"She's okay," Officer Reagan assured him. "Just scared, that's all. She's back home, safe and sound."

"Back from where?" he insisted.

"She'll tell you about it." He gave Dad a reprimanding frown. "Our kids need guidance. And good examples." Then tipping his hat, he delivered his final words of wisdom. "Take my advice, Laura. Get those stars out of your eyes. Goodnight, now."

Officer Reagan closed the door behind us.

I stood there, staring into the angry face of my father, hoping I'd faint!

Chapter 16

I won't spare the gory details.

How and why was Dad there? I'll tell you.

He'd gotten a call from one of his accounts, asking him to deliver the artwork he'd completed. Naturally, Dad called to say he was driving down that evening. He didn't get an answer. Getting to the city, naturally, he called Mrs. Hallifax. He didn't get an answer. He asked the doorman when she'd return. Naturally, Larry told Dad she'd taken Sarah to Florida days before. Then Dad sat around the house, *waiting* for me. Was I dead in the street, mugged, kidnapped? Afraid to call Mom and tell her I'd disappeared, he called my friends in the city. Naturally, they were all out of town. That's when he almost called the police, but kept hoping I'd return before morning.

So he sat up and waited. No wonder he was furious!

But Dad's a strange guy. When he really gets angry, he dosn't blow up; he shuts up.

"Are you all right?" he asked.

I nodded.

"You weren't hurt, mugged or kidnapped?"

I nodded.

"Then whatever you did tonight was your fault and no one else's?"

Again, I nodded.

"In that case, Laura, I'm too angry to discuss it. I'm going to bed now, and we'll deal with it tomorrow."

Dad always tries not to act in anger. It may be good for him, but it was *awful* for me. As exhausted as I was, I couldn't get to sleep. I lay awake, wondering what Dad had planned for me. What would he do when he learned everything? Should I tell the whole truth or fudge a little? No, I was in a big enough mess; I'd better be honest. But what would he say when he discovered the details?

I lay there worrying about it. And I'll bet Dad knew that. He was getting even for the hours he'd worried over me. (Parents can be sneaky sometimes.)

Around nine o'clock, I heard Dad in the kitchen and followed him out. At last we could clear the air .

"Laura, where's the food? There's nothing here but moldy garlic and onions."

147

"There's no food, Dad. Can we talk now?"

"No," he said sharply. "I'm going out for breakfast. Then I'm delivering my work. Be back at noon. But don't you dare leave the house!"'

So I spent another three hours worrying about my fate. By the time Dad returned, I was ready to spill my guts! (I told you parents were sneaky.)

I confessed every gruesome detail, sparing myself nothing. Halfway through my story, I was convinced that Dad had taken pity on me. I'd suffered enough. My dreams of fame were shattered. My magic dress was ruined. What worse punishment was there?

Dad listened patiently, then asked, "Well, Laura, what've you learned from this experience?"

Can you believe such a stupid question!

He sounded like Glinda the Good Witch asking Dorothy what she'd learned in Oz, because she couldn't return to Kansas until she knew. Well, I hadn't learned anything! But obviously Dad expected me to rattle off some profound over-the-rainbow wisdom.

Well, all I knew was that it had been a horribly disappointing experience, and I wanted to forget it.

"This isn't school, Dad. I don't know what I learned. I just feel awful."

"School's a small learning experience, Laura. Life's the big one. There's no point in feeling awful if you can't gain something from it."

"Well I can't! The whole thing's unfair. I'm sorry if

I worried you, and I apologize for that. But I didn't do anything wrong, and I still want to be in that movie."

Dad sighed disappointedly. "I'm sorry you feel that way. Get packed. We're driving back to Windham. You'll have to repeat this for your mother. We have no secrets in this family."

I could tell Dad was disgusted. But he didn't say another word. I was given the silent treatment for three hours in the car.

Mom was thrilled to see me.

"Laura, what a surprise. We didn't expect you till Saturday. Did you get time off? Did you enjoy yourself?"

"Save your questions," said Dad solemnly. "You'll have new ones soon. Laura's got something to tell you."

"Let the punishment fit the crime." Who said that, Gilbert or Sullivan? Believe me, there's no worse punishment than having to confess your sins in front of a stinky seven-year-old sister!

We weren't in the house more than minutes before Dad insisted we all sit down so I could spill my guts again.

Actually, I didn't mind telling Mom. Surely, she'd give me the sympathy Dad hadn't.

Wrong!

"Laura, you got drunk? How could you? You told us lies? How could you?"

Crissy sat smugly. "Mom was right. You *have* gone nuts!"

"Can't you think about how *I* feel?" I asked. "*My* heartache? *My* disappointment?"

"My daughter, Mom moaned. "Dragged home by the police! Laura, how *could* you?"

I'd finished groveling! "It wasn't easy!" I shouted, getting up from the sofa.

Mom was stunned. "Aren't you sorry for what you did? Scaring your father to death? Abusing our confidence? Haven't you learned a lesson?"

"No I haven't! Punish me if you like, but I haven't learned anything."

Dad tried retaining the cool for which he's famous. "Laura, go to your room."

"Gladly. When you think of a punishment disgusting enough, let me know. Until then, leave me alone!"

Storming into my room had dramatic flair, but it was a flop.

I had no room. In my absence, Crissy had commandeered every inch of it. Her books and toys were scattered all over the place. And Boris Baboon had my bed!

There were pads, notebooks, piles of typing paper all over the place. Bunches of letters and piles of notes were tacked on the wall: send to Peter . . . private stuff . . . maybe stories . . . That kid had turned the place into a writing factory!

I pushed all her junk into a lump and threw Boris aside. While I was propping a chair up against the door, Crissy came storming through. She took one look at her papers scattered around and turned purple.

"You stinker! What'd you do that for? I had them all in order. Peter's waiting for my story, and now you've mixed things up."

"I don't care. This is my room, too."

Her lower lip quivered, but she wouldn't give me the satisfaction of crying. Instead, she gathered up her papers, picked Boris from the floor, then stood with her pile of junk, staring at me.

"You're not a nice person, Laura. And you're a *rotten* sister!"

Sticking her nose in the air, she left the room.

I threw myself on the bed and began to cry.

For the next few days, Crissy steered clear of me. So did Mom and Dad. I was a pariah, an untouchable to be avoided for fear of contamination. This was part of my folks' brilliant scheme to make me "think." But I wasn't buying it.

Let them ignore me; I didn't care. As far as I could see, things were exactly the same as before. Mom and Dad were busy with their work, and Crissy with her stories.

So I returned to the old TV. Phoebe still had her drinking problem, Harriet still had amnesia, and Marsha hadn't figured out who the heck she was.

I'd lay on the deck whenever the sun came up, soaking up the rays. Sometimes, Dad came out and sat down beside me, trying to get into conversation. But it always got back to the same thing: what've you learned. My answer was always the same: nothing.

It was making me nervous. I still hadn't been punished and the threat of it hung over my head like a water bucket about to drop. And I told him so.

"Listen, Dad, rip out my nails, send me to Siberia, but tell me how to clear things up."

"That answer's got to come from you, Laura. I'm treating you as an adult."

"Well, treat me like a kid, and let's get this over."

Dad made that awful disappointed sigh. "It's not that easy. But you'll figure it out—in time."

Terrific, right? I tell you, parents sure know how to make you feel like a nerd!

One day, while I was still deep in my black funk, Mom decided to become domestic. She'd finished her magazine articles and had a craving to putter in the kitchen. This meant homemade soup. Mom considers it as life-restoring as penicillin.

Whistling her head off, she spent the afternoon cutting, chopping and dicing. The chickens and vegetables cooked on the stove all day, while the rain poured down outside. By dinnertime, Crissy and Dad were drooling. They rushed to the table, breaking off great hunks of hot buttered bread, anxious to dunk them into the broth.

I wasn't hungry. I missed my fresh cucumbers and lovely crystal bowl of strawberries. Watching everyone plunk those hot cooked vegetables in their bowls made me sick.

"Laura," said Mom, "you're not eating. It's homemade."

"I don't care." I sighed. "Fresh vegetables are more nutritious."

Dad finally lost his cool. "Sit down at this table," he ordered.

"I won't," I said, pushing open the terrace door and letting the rain pour in.

"Then go outside and stay there," he shouted. "Maybe the rain'll clear your head." Slamming the door behind me, he returned to his dinner.

I didn't care. Let them sit warm and cozy indoors, while I stood miserable and unwanted. Let them feed their faces while my soul starved. Maybe I'd get pneumonia; then they'd be sorry. I'd be like Camille, lying on a sickbed of organdy and lace, wasting away to nothing.

The wind blew wildly across my face, hurling wet strings of hair against my cheeks. Staring sadly across the mountains, I thought of all those delicate beauties who'd been abandoned in their hour of pain. Those wonderful movie heroines who'd loved and lost and never learned to love again.

. . . I was Scarlett, standing in the doorway, begging Rhett to come back.

. . . I was Cathy, standing on the desolate moors, waiting for my lover, Heathcliff.

. . . I was Laura . . . yes, still Laura, the face in the misty mountain light.

And I couldn't help thinking what a beautifully romantic picture I'd make!

Chapter 17

With only two days of vacation left, my folks started to panic. They began rushing around, doing all the things they could have done all summer: walks in the woods, mountain climbing, nature hikes, determined to suck the juices from those last few days.

I didn't join in. I was happy for the time alone. After all, I was the only friend I had!

One afternoon when they'd left and I was looking through the latest *Seventeen* magazine for the seventeenth time, someone rang the bell.

I was surprised to see that it was Peter. I hadn't seen him for years, but recognized him immediately. He stood in the doorway, wearing jogging shorts, sneakers and a backpack. His long hair was tied in a pony tail, and he'd grown a beard.

"Didn't Crissy tell you I was coming?" he asked, noticing my expression.

"No, we don't talk much lately."

"I know," he nodded.

"Come in. What brings you here?"

"I was visiting friends in Tannersville and promised Crissy I'd drop by."

"This way," I said. "Our living room's upstairs."

"I know. Crissy told me."

"I bet that's not all she told you. Crissy's been writing down every dumb thing that's happened all summer. That kid's bonkers about your contest. She must write you every day."

"Not quite." He smiled. "It's wonderful having a student like Crissy. She's so alive to everything and does fantastic work. Her story about mountain mice was an amazing allegory."

I could see that Peter hadn't changed; just as peculiar as ever.

"Yeah, well she snoops, too. Was that your idea?" (Normally, I'd never talk to a teacher like that. But strictly speaking, Peter wasn't a teacher. Besides, he was different. I'd always considered him more like a child than an adult. And he liked one-to-one relationships and encouraged kids to treat him like a ten-year-old!)

"Crissy's still a little confused between snooping and observing." He smiled some more.

I poured us some lemonade. "Is this contest really

such a big deal? Crissy talks about it as if it were the Nobel Prize."

"It is, to the kids. Our Writer's Collaborative has a special grant this year. We're printing five students' work."

"Oh, I remember those little booklets when I was in school."

"No, this is different," he said excitedly. "A professional printing job. The books'll be marketed like real paperbacks. We've made arrangements with bookshops to sell them. We've set a publication date, an autographing party in a local store: the works."

(Listening to Peter describe the project, he sounded like a ten-year-old.)

"That's pretty exciting," I admitted.

"Of course, the printings will be small—a few hundred copies each. But we'll be giving the most talented kids professional exposure."

"And I suppose Crissy's one of them? She's hard enough to live with. Now she'll be impossible."

"That's what I came to see her about. Crissy has a flair for humor. Her drawings are filled with symbolism, and her anthropomorphic twist is charming."

"Sounds like a disease."

"The baboon symbolism," he explained. "Haven't you read it?"

I sipped my lemonade. "Crissy's always writing something. I don't pay attention."

"But you must," Peter insisted, taking a manila

envelope from his backpack. "Recognition within one's own family is always important."

He was telling me? I could tell him a thing or two!

Peter handed me the book Crissy had mailed him. She'd drawn lots of little pictures and pasted them above the title, "Baboons in the Country." It sounded sappy to me, and I was sick of hearing about Boris.

Well, this particular little fable wasn't about Boris, but about a far more familiar bunch of baboons. I didn't read long before I decided that Crissy would soon have a fat lip!

Her little epic told of the baboon family's adventures in the mountains one summer, complete with illustrations. Mother Baboon had a big behind, which she stuffed into faded jeans. Father Baboon wore ink-splattered shirts and had a paintbrush stuck through his nose. And Big Sister Baboon wore a large straw hat and two powder puffs glued to her cheeks.

That bratty kid had spared no one! Her story was filled with the most intimate details of our private lives. Father Baboon slept in dirty underwear. Mother Baboon burped when she ate onions and left clumps of chewed-up gum stuck to her typewriter. And Big Sister Baboon pasted pictures of herself over other baboons in fashion magazines.

Oh yes, Big Sister Baboon was the biggest dope of all; running around getting drunk in baboon bars and trying to push her way into baboon movies.

Sound familiar? Well, it got worse as I continued reading:

One day, Big Sister Baboon fell over a camera in the woods. "I'm a star!" she cried. She ran to the Baboon Boutique, bought lots of silly clothes, then moved to New York City. Mother Baboon, happy to see her go, rented out her room to a famous little baboon writer, who wrote lots of wonderful stories ever after . . .

There was more, but I didn't bother reading it. Oh, it was funny and well-written, but if Peter planned to print it, I planned to sue!

"What nerve!" I shouted.

"Don't you think it's funny?'

"As a crutch. Aren't there laws to protect people from this?"

"You mean censorship?" He frowned. "Writers have fought that for centuries: Emile Zola, D. H. Lawrence, Henry Miller."

"Well, those guys didn't have sisters. I have rights too, don't I?'

Peter was about to sink into a deep literary discussion when Crissy and my parents returned. Crissy's eyes lit up when she saw him.

"Did you like my story?"

"Very much."

"Then you'll print it?" she squealed. "Oh, I

knew I'd be famous someday!" Spinning around in my direction, she stuck her tongue out gleefully.

"We're so proud of you," said Mom.

"Now we have *two* writers in the family." Dad beamed.

Fuming inside, I said nothing.

Peter suddenly looked uneasy. "I'm sorry, Crissy. We're not printing your story."

As Crissy's face fell a mile, I couldn't help smirking. Peter wasn't so peculiar after all.

"It wasn't an easy decision," he said hesitantly. "With only five choices, we can print only the best. I'm afraid this story isn't Crissy's best."

Now it was my turn to gloat. "Too bad," I said sarcastically.

"But I thought you liked it," said Crissy.

"It was charming, light and funny. But you can do better."

"How can you know that?" asked Dad.

"I wouldn't have," Peter explained. "Not if Crissy hadn't sent me something else. I found it stuffed inside her book." He handed Crissy a pile of papers.

"But these are my *secret* thoughts," she said. "I didn't mean to mail that."

Secret thoughts? Crissy's baboon story revealed more than enough. What juicy items were on *those* pages? Dynamite, no doubt. While I wondered about that, Crissy looked confused, and Mom and Dad looked angry. They stared at Peter as if he'd murdered someone.

"Let me explain," he said awkwardly. "Our standards must be the highest. The kids who win will be treated like professionals. The day of publication, they'll appear on the local news. The stores will charge two dollars per copy for their books. That money goes back into the cooperative, to help publish again. So you see, it's very competitive. Crissy, your story is good, but your journal is better. If you work harder, I'm sure you can turn it into something fine. Then maybe we'll publish it next year."

"Next year?" She groaned.

"But she's worked so hard already," said Mom.

"I know that, Mrs. Andrews. But she'll have to work harder; just as a professional would. Besides, all the children publishing are much older. So if Crissy waits until next year, she'll still be the youngest author in print."

"Hear that, honey?" Mom smiled. "You'll be the youngest."

"That's still pretty special," said Dad.

"I guess so," she muttered.

Mom asked Peter to stay for dinner while Crissy sat in glum silence.

I had to hand it to my kid sister; she gets over disappointment fast. All during dinner, Peter kept repeating how much faith he had in Crissy's potential. Then he carried on about her dumb story, "filled with simian symbolism."

Crissy smiled politely. She didn't eat much, but she didn't seem upset. Little kids get over stuff so fast!

As for me, I was relieved that the story of Big Sister Baboon wouldn't see the light of day. I could imagine the field day my friends would have if they ever read it. Gloria Goggins would buy her own spot on the local news to personally advertise it to the world!

Still, I was curious. Peter liked the story but thought Crissy's journals were better. He kept saying how "honest and sensitive" they were. Just how honest I wondered? I couldn't wait to read them. Maybe she'd get a fat lip, after all!

As soon as Peter left, Crissy went to her room and I went looking for her notes. Finding them on the coffee-table, I took them to the terrace to read. There were a stack of them, scribbled on loose leaf paper and all about the family.

There was one about Dad:

> I wonder if Daddy wishes one of us was a boy.
> I know he's always wanted one. I guess being
> girls doesn't make Daddy love us less. But
> would being boys make him love us more?

And one about Mom:

I like to watch Mom work. Her face screws up all funny and serious. I love the sound of her typewriter, making words pop out on the pages. Someday, I'll write words that pop like firecrackers. A big explosion of words that make people happy.

And several about me:

It's sad to see grownups cry. Teenagers aren't finished growing, but that's sad, too. I heard Laura cry last night. She's not going to be a famous movie star. She's not going to be anything. It must be awful to find out you're nothing. Laura worries about it a lot. Sometimes, I see sad things in her face. She tries to act grownup, so people won't notice. She sits in the corner, staring out the window. I think she's pretending she's a fancy lady. But she doesn't look fancy. She looks hurt and sad.

I read another:

Laura didn't eat her soup last night. Daddy got mad and let her stand in the rain. She came in all cold and wet with a scary look in her eyes. I hope she doesn't hate us all. It's awful to have someone hate you. Does Laura think we

163

hate her? That must be worse. I try being nice to her, but she says such mean things. So I leave her alone. But maybe that's what makes her sad and lonely.

There were lots more pages, mainly about me. Reading through them, I got a peculiar feeling. I had had no idea Crissy spent so much time analyzing me. I had been comfortable having a feisty kid sister with a heart of steel and didn't care for her sudden deep insights into my personality, no matter how accurate. Wasn't it bad enough she'd made me into a baboon? Must she pick my brain, too? Now I'd have to add Peter to the list of people who considered me a nut, along with Gloria and Larry. Pretty soon all New York would know what a jerk I'd been!

All the same, Crissy had had a lousy disappointment, and I was the first to know how that felt. Maybe a few words from someone else with battle scars might help.

I went downstairs and passed by the bedroom door. It was closed, but I could hear Crissy crying inside. I felt like going in to tell her how sorry I was about her bum deal. But I didn't.

What the heck. She wouldn't have believed me anyway.

Chapter 18

I slept on the sofa that night, not wanting to deal with a sobby little sister. The next morning Crissy came to breakfast, her eyes all puffy. She grabbed a bowl of cereal and in stoic silence returned to her room.

Mom began cleaning and packing for our return to the city, and Dad started stuffing the car. I hung around reading the local papers, where I noticed an article that said Camp Wachanawa had closed for the summer the day before.

I packed my lunch and my transistor and took the afternoon bus to Tannersville. My body cried out for water, and for the first time all summer, the lake was empty. I dived in, swam out to the center, then floated around in privacy. Swimming always helps me clear my head, and somehow, I was hoping that being alone out there I'd suddenly begin making some sense of my disastrous summer.

But it was no use. The entire summer had been senseless. Woody Allen had scrapped a perfectly good movie because it was too funny. Crissy had lost an important contest because her story was too cute. People were shooting an absolutely horrible film by the Boat Basin, when they should've been making a beautiful love story. And I, still certain I was destined for Cinderella fame, was nothing more than a pumpkin.

I dried myself off, stretched out on the beach and stared out at the mountains. They were already beginning to turn into the reds and brown of autumn. Another summer was slowly dying.

I switched on the radio and heard an old Roger Miller number. Lying back, I listened to the lyrics:

> You can't roller skate in a buffalo herd,
> You can't take a shave in a parakeet cage,
> But you can be happy if you've a mind to.
> You can be happy if you put your mind to it.
> Buckle down, knuckle down, do it, do it.

Ha! Who can be happy when life makes no sense? When dreams and Dream Dresses are so easily destroyed.

Still, I supposed if there was one Dream Dress in the world, there might be another. And I had been Cinderella for a short while. I could still recall how that soft silk felt against my skin, the confidence it filled me with. Models must feel that way all the time, constantly wearing the most beautiful fashions. I guess I had my memories . . .

. . . *Knuckle down, buckle down, do it, do it . . .*

. . . Do what, I wondered? Make the best of a bad experience? I could write Woody Allen a poison-pen letter, telling him how he'd ruined my life. I'd mail him the raggy remnants of Dream Dress and ask for restitution.

Or I could find out where he lived, sneak into his apartment and beg him to put me back in his movie.

Then again, I could forget the whole darned thing!

But I didn't want to forget the good parts. The fun I had had shopping. The excursions with Sarah. Dreams of acting and modeling still pulled at me. Of course, I could always stop dreaming and start working at it. Become a *real* model, maybe? Make the rounds of agencies after school. Perhaps take a modeling course. Mom and Dad might finance that, if my schoolwork improved. I might even take acting lessons. There were lots of good professional schools in the city. In fact, Mom might approve of all that hard work and study. Top models take acting classes, too. It was a possibility . . .

. . . *No, you can't roller skate in a buffalo herd,*
   But you can be happy if you've a mind to.

I switched off the radio, went for another swim and watched the sunlight play against the lily pads. A dragonfly resting on the wet white petals looked translucent through the sunlight. White clouds raced across the sky, creating shadows along the mountains. Patches of lush red and gold glowed brightly, while faint tinges of purple shadows darkened the higher peaks. Autumn might not be so bad, after all.

Shivering, I swam back to shore, threw on my sweatshirt and said goodbye to the mountains, wondering if we'd ever be back this way again.

As I sat on the bench at Main Street, waiting for the bus, I watched the cars passing by. Lots of them were packed with children, bikes and cardboard cartons. Families had closed up their summer houses and were returning to the city, all ready to begin a new season. For me, the old one still seemed oddly unfinished.

The sun had turned a copper color by the time I returned home. Hiking up the long dirt path to the house, I felt strangely quiet inside.

Dad was still packing the car, trying to find a spot for the cow's skull he'd discovered in the woods. Its sleek white bones had been picked clean, and he planned to use it for a series of charcoal sketches. Mom was still in the kitchen, scrubbing down cabinets and packing up food cartons. She'd merely reversed the process she'd gone through two months before. And Crissy was in the bedroom, pounding away at her typewriter. I glanced at her title page: "The Heartaches of a Youth."

Yes, everyone was doing their own thing, as usual. Nothing had changed. Life always seemed to have its busy beavers and its dreamers. But sometimes artists and writers were dreamers, too. So were actors. And maybe even models.

Sighing, I carefully folded my clothes and put them in my suitcase. At least I was going back to Bloomies. That was a help. As I stacked up my fashion magazines, I thought again about the possibility of modeling or acting school. Maybe I'd have a long talk with Mom and Dad about it when we returned to the city.

I didn't know. Maybe you could be happy, if you had a mind to. But just then, feeling nothing seemed, strangely, to satisfy me.

Like Scarlett O'Hara, I'd think about it all again tomorrow.